She'd ... and she'd taken him

"Whatever gave me the idea I was the one in control?" Nick asked, rolling off Blair. Even in the bright sun, he suddenly felt cold, so he pulled her on top of him, pleased when she snuggled her face into his chest and draped her legs around his thighs.

"Control is a figment of the imagination," she said smoothly. "And losing it is kind of exciting, too."

He would have laughed, but he was too exhausted. "We're going to get sunburned," he commented lazily.

"I don't see what *you're* worried about." Blair stretched her legs before resettling them around his. "There's nothing of *you* for the sun to get a peek at."

"That's true," he said, "but if you hand me the lotion, I'll take care of your tender parts."

Blair felt a thrill race through her as he spoke. She needed a rest, a nap even, but obviously her body had other ideas....

Emma Jane Spenser is a bright new star for Harlequin. Her first Temptation, *A Novel Approach*, garnered rave reviews when it hit the stands last April, and we think *That Holiday Feeling* will establish Emma Jane as a "must-read" author.

Sensuous, funny, exotic and moving— *That Holiday Feeling* has it all! You'll particularly enjoy the colorful European settings, the details of which are drawn from Emma Jane's memories of living abroad with her husband and young son.

Books by Emma Jane Spenser
HARLEQUIN TEMPTATION
248–A NOVEL APPROACH

Don't miss any of our special offers. Write to us at the following address for information on our newest releases.

Harlequin Reader Service
901 Fuhrmann Blvd., P.O. Box 1397, Buffalo, NY 14240
Canadian address: P.O. Box 603,
Fort Erie, Ont. L2A 5X3

That Holiday Feeling

EMMA JANE SPENSER

Harlequin Books

TORONTO • NEW YORK • LONDON
AMSTERDAM • PARIS • SYDNEY • HAMBURG
STOCKHOLM • ATHENS • TOKYO • MILAN

For Shar

Published November 1989

ISBN 0-373-25373-7

1

STANDING IN THE SHADOWS beneath the blackened timber supports that ran the length of the alpine stube, Nick caught his breath when she smiled. Not meant for him—or anyone else in the room—the smile lit up her eyes, making them sparkle in the wavering candlelight. Then, as if she suddenly sensed his need to breathe, she lowered her lashes, hiding the light of her amusement from the people around her.

He recovered slowly, savoring the remnants of tension her smile had provoked. It had happened before, the smile . . . and the tension. Just a few moments ago he'd looked up from reading the paper to catch her laughing quietly, unself-consciously sharing a joke with herself, completely indifferent to the reactions of people around her. She was daydreaming, he realized. Or maybe just dreaming.

It had hit him hard then, her smile, punching him in the gut when he least expected it. Afterward, he'd waited, preparing himself this time, knowing that without the element of surprise, the jolt would be minimized.

He'd been wrong.

It hit him harder than before. The assault filled his senses, made him want to close the distance to her table and drag her into his arms. And once he did that, there would be no stopping.

Nick stared hard, daring her to look up from her contemplation of the small, bright flame that flickered erratically at the top of the brass candlestick. But she didn't, and he began to breathe easier. Perhaps it was for the best. His heart wasn't quite ready for another jolt.

She had come in alone, and from the look of things, she intended to stay alone. Several of the male guests had tried to change that, and Nick could understand their attraction. She was a lovely woman. Not beautiful like a model, but comfortably pretty with finely drawn features, wide-set eyes and reddish-blond hair that lightly brushed her shoulders in a style that was casually messy. It looked sexy, as if she'd just climbed out of bed. It suited her that way, and he could almost feel the silky curls clinging to his fingers.

It was hard to tell much about her figure under the bulky après-ski clothes, but Nick found his imagination doing overtime on that one. Then he watched as yet another man approached her, only to be turned away with a firm shake of her head that was softened by a smile.

Perhaps there was a man waiting for her…in the next room, in the next town.

Or maybe there wasn't.

Either way, Nick intended to find out everything there was to know. But first he had to get close enough to ask. Considering the number of men she'd rebuffed in the past few minutes, the odds were against him.

Nick *never* let himself be swayed by the odds.

Crossing his fingers that she spoke English, he set the empty beer mug on the bar and threaded his way through the scattered tables until he stood beside her chair. He waited then, respecting her privacy. It was like knocking before entering a room.

Finally, after one of those short moments that seemed like an eternity, she tilted her head and lifted her lashes so that he could see her eyes. Nick hesitated. It wasn't easy to remember what he'd intended to say when she focused her gaze on him . . . and nothing else. He felt as if he was the only person in her world, at least for the moment.

Perhaps he had a chance after all. "I'd like—"

"*Mom!*"

The interruption was loud and clear, and Nick stopped speaking to search nearby tables for evidence of a child to match the voice. A quick glance left him puzzled. There were no children in the bar.

His eyes darted back to the woman who was extracting a bulky object from a deep pocket.

"Excuse me," she said politely, then proceeded to speak into the walkie-talkie. "No need to shout, love. I'm not on another planet, just down the hall."

"*So turn down the volume, Mom,*" responded the voice.

Nick experienced a pang of disappointment. She had a child, and probably a husband. But a quick check of her left hand showed no signs of a wedding ring. He considered the ramifications of that, then pulled out a chair and sat down.

Blair was so startled that she nearly forgot Taylor at the other end of the walkie-talkie. Startled, but not overly concerned. She could take care of him after she was finished talking with her daughter.

"What's the problem, Taylor?"

"I can't find Peter Rabbit."

Blair stared into space as she thought about it, then suddenly realized she was attracting a fair amount of attention from the people at nearby tables. Belatedly she turned the volume lower. "Have you tried the refrigerator?"

"The refrigerator?"

With more confidence, Blair continued. "Peter was helping me get your milk earlier." And she vaguely remembered setting the stuffed toy down so she could open the seal on the bottle.

"I'll go check," her daughter said.

In that vacuum of silence, she let her gaze drift back to the stranger sitting quietly beside her. He had an interesting face, she thought idly. Attractive without being handsome. His straight, sandy-brown hair was cut short at the neckline but left longer on top—neat without being styled. Thick, dark eyebrows called attention to equally dark eyes. She liked his eyes, particularly the lazy way they were watching her without making her feel as if she were under a microscope. High cheekbones rose above the faint shadows that signaled a heavy beard, and she wondered what he would look like if he quit shaving for just a few days. The image excited her, although she couldn't imagine why. She'd never even touched a man's beard.

But it was the frankly sensual mouth that fascinated her. She let her eyes linger there, tracing the pattern of his lips from corner to corner, knowing they would be firm to the touch. Firm and hot.

"He's cold, Mom."

Taylor was back. Blair squeezed her eyes closed, putting her imagination on hold. "He'll get over it, love. Now go to bed. Time's almost up."

"If he catches cold . . ."

"Trust me, Taylor," she interrupted. "He won't catch cold. But *you'll* catch something if you're not asleep in precisely ten minutes," she threatened, checking the time on her watch.

"'Night, Mom."

"Good night, Taylor," she said softly, then slipped the portable radio back into her pocket.

"Peter Rabbit is . . . ?" the stranger began slowly, leaving her an opening she had to fill.

"Stuffed."

"But in the refrigerator?" he asked, a single brow lifting in amusement.

Blair shrugged, refusing to be embarrassed. "At least I remembered," she said, deftly excusing her behavior. "Last time he was stuck in my tennis bag for three days before we found him."

"I'll bet he was relieved. When you found him, that is," he continued, daring her to tell him the rest.

"He smelled like my socks. I had to toss him in the washing machine. Twice," she admitted, finding she liked the sound of the stranger's voice as much as she liked watching his mouth form the words. His accent was a fascinating mixture of midwestern drawl and East Coast twang. She waited for him to say something else.

"I suspect the cure for frostbite is less drastic," he said, referring to the rabbit's confinement in the refrigerator.

"As long as he doesn't smell like leftover pizza," Blair commented, suddenly remembering the box they'd brought from the restaurant. "I don't think he'd survive another bout with the tumble dryer."

He grinned, and she answered with a smile that reflected her own enjoyment. He was amusing, this stranger. And she liked watching him. His face was expressive. And honest.

He had the look of a successful man. She couldn't define how she could tell just by looking, but it was there...the unmistakable air of a man who had climbed the ladder of success and was committed to preserving the status he'd attained.

Unfortunately, as far as Blair was concerned, that was *not* an asset. In her experience, it took supreme dedication to a career in order to achieve and maintain that high level of success. In short, you had to be a workaholic to succeed...and stay there.

The signs were easily recognizable—especially for an ex-workaholic like herself. And the man sitting beside her showed telltale symptoms.

Blair made it a point to avoid workaholics. They made her nervous.

Still, it was only a suspicion... Maybe just a few minutes wouldn't hurt.

"I'm Nicholas Dalton. My friends call me Nick."

He held out his hand, and she put her own into it. It was warm there. She hated to end the greeting. "Blair. Blair Forrest. My daughter and I just arrived this morning." Gently she withdrew her hand.

"I know."

His voice rumbled, she decided. He didn't just talk, he rumbled. She could feel the deep, husky notes calling her spine to attention. It was unlike any sensation she'd ever experienced.

She liked it.

"You saw us arrive?" she asked, knowing he hadn't. She would have remembered if he'd been there that morning. Even with all the confusion of checking in and rushing out to the slopes, she would have remembered.

He shook his head. "No, I missed that."

And he sounded as though he regretted it. Blair liked that, just as she liked the way he was still watching her, as if he was drinking in every word and expression. He projected an almost greedy fascination.

The feeling was mutual.

"So how...?" she asked, biting her lip in puzzlement then watching as his eyes dropped to her lips. That made her nervous. Not nervous as in frightened or spooked, but nervous as in excited.

"It's a small pension. If you'd been here last night, I would have seen you." Then, almost as an afterthought, he continued. "You weren't in the dining room tonight. I wouldn't have missed that."

Blair gulped. He made it sound as though it was a personal loss. "We had some shopping to do. Then Taylor saw the place that advertised American pizza."

"Ah, yes. Taylor. The voice with the rabbit."

"My daughter. She's eleven," she said simply. "I don't like leaving her alone, but she can't get to sleep if I'm roaming around the room. She says I'm too noisy," she added, disbelief clear in her expression. Patting the walkie-talkie in her pocket, she said, "This is a compromise."

"Eleven? Isn't that kind of old for a stuffed animal?"

"Not really," she replied. "Besides, her boyfriend won it for her at the fête last month and she's kind of attached to it."

"Boyfriend? At her age?" What was an eleven-year-old doing with a boyfriend, he wondered, seriously doubting the judgment of her mother.

"André's nine," Blair countered, lifting her eyebrows in amusement at his disapproval.

Nick relaxed somewhat. "Better than falling for an older man."

"Absolutely," she said, and nodded in agreement. Then, leaning slightly forward to signal an air of secrecy, she added, "Confidentially, I suspect he won it for himself and was too embarrassed to carry Peter home."

"I didn't think boys that age were into girls yet," he commented.

"Not usually. I get the feeling that as soon as André realizes Taylor's a girl—" She wordlessly finished the sentence by making a dramatic slicing motion against her throat.

"He doesn't know?"

"We're talking about 'Tomboy Taylor,' heroine of the football team, fastest sprinter in the gang, not to mention the best net-ball player in Bruges," Blair said with pride, warming to the subject. "She's just beginning to discover the difference between boys and girls for herself."

He grinned, finally understanding the nature of Taylor's relationship with André. Just as important, he was discovering all sorts of important stuff about Blair. Such as how her eyes shone when she talked about her daughter. How she used her hands to make a point, and how quickly her mind worked.

And how much he wanted to know her better.

Blair suddenly noticed his gaze was fastened on her hand. The left one, where the ring was supposed to be . . . if she'd had one. He kept it there for a moment, then lifted his eyes to meet hers. The question was there. By not voicing it, he was forcing her to make a decision. If she simply ignored the question, he'd back away. Is that what she wanted?

She hesitated, though she didn't know why. He was really asking a simple, logical question. So why, she wondered, did it feel like she was making a commitment?

Shifting uneasily in her chair, she opted for the easy way out. "Taylor and I are here alone."

"That doesn't answer the question," he pointed out silkily.

"I'm not sure it's important," she hedged, wondering if things were getting out of control or if she was just out of practice.

"It is to me," he said. "I'm not married, and I don't go around asking married women to have dinner with me."

"I'm not married," she admitted finally. His persistence surprised her, especially in view of the fact that he knew she was here with a child. She generally found that men weren't nearly as interested in her once they found out about Taylor.

He smiled then, a slow smile that warmed her deep inside. "So how about dinner?"

Regretfully she reminded him about the pizza. "I don't think there's room left for more. Besides, I have to get back to Taylor."

"I was thinking about tomorrow night."

Torn by indecision, she pretended not to hear him. Instead she glanced at her watch and took a last gulp of the wine. "I'm late. Taylor will be worried."

"Taylor is supposed to be asleep," he reminded her gently, not the least put off by her evasion.

"You're right, of course," she said brightly, jumping up from the table. "And I'm dead on my feet. I think I'll have an early night."

"About dinner...?" Nick pushed his chair away from the table and stood.

She was tempted. For the first time in ages, Blair felt the need to say yes. But there was Taylor to consider. This was *their* holiday. "Sorry," she said, hiding the regret with difficulty. "I really can't."

And then, before he had a chance to argue, she slipped away from the table and out the door.

Nick didn't try to follow her. Instead he settled back in the cushioned chair and signaled for another beer. Pulling a well-worn map of the ski area from his pocket, he studied the mountain, charting his route for the following day.

He could always ask her again in the morning.

WHY DIDN'T YOU SAY YES? Blair asked herself for the tenth time. Brushing her teeth with punishing vigor, she stared angrily into the mirror and demanded an answer.

Taylor was an excuse, and not even a valid one. Her daughter had been badgering her to go out with someone—*anyone*—for ages now. Ever since her school friend's single mother had begun to date last fall, Taylor had been pestering Blair to do the same. It was no use explaining that she hadn't really met anyone who interested her enough to spend time away from her daughter. Taylor didn't buy that argument. With the precocious wisdom of a child, she pointed out that Blair couldn't possibly decide whether or not she liked someone if she didn't give him a chance.

Blair reached for the brush and pulled it through her hair, grimacing in uncharacteristic frustration after just a few strokes. The natural wave in her hair gave it a mind of its own, and she had long since given up doing more than coaxing it into reasonable order. But tonight the wild disarray bothered her, not because it looked any different, but because she was suddenly self-conscious about everything.

Slamming the brush onto the vanity, she winced at the loud noise it made in the quiet room and guiltily peeked at Taylor's bed. The body under the covers didn't budge, and she breathed easier. Taking care to move quietly, Blair crossed the room to her own bed and reached down to flick off the bedside light. In the abrupt darkness, she pulled off her clothes and slipped under the thick duvet.

Shivering as the rough sheets settled around her body, she hugged her knees to her chest and willed the involuntary shaking to stop. The cold was distracting. She couldn't think about anything except getting warm.

Nick could make her warm, she thought, trembling violently at the image of his tall, lean body curved against her own. He would be hard. And strong. Even under the bulky ski sweater, the broad shoulders had a powerful look to them. Nothing flashy, but a manly strength that excited her.

So why hadn't she said yes?

The covers were warm now, and in the never-never land just before sleep, Blair hoped he would ask again.

2

"SO WHERE IS EVERYONE, MOM?" Taylor asked. In the silence of the nearly empty dining room, her words seemed to bounce off the walls.

"Not everybody gets up with the sun, Taylor," Blair said dryly.

"Don't they know the best skiing is first thing in the morning?" her daughter asked.

"Think about it, love. The best skiing is in the morning *because* everyone else is still asleep," she pointed out with a grin. "And it's one of the best kept secrets of the sport, so keep your voice down."

Taylor giggled, then picked up her roll and spread it thickly with soft cheese and butter. "Do you think we'll get lost again today?" she asked before taking a huge bite.

"Probably. Worried?"

"Naw," her daughter replied, busily preparing another roll as she nibbled on the first. Cutting the bread in half, she spread cheese and added the thinly sliced salami before wrapping the sandwich in a napkin. "Want me to make you one?" she asked. "Just in case we get *really* lost?"

Blair nodded. It never hurt to be prepared. There were numerous huts offering food and drink on the mountain, but they tended to be overcrowded at lunchtime. They could eat sandwiches anywhere at all, followed by soup or goulash when the huts cleared out.

Besides, there was always the chance they'd never see one of the huts. Skiing without a map had its hazards.

"Hurry up, Mom!" Taylor prodded, anxious to get going. "The ski bus to the gondola will pass by any minute now."

"For someone who's only been here one day, you seem to know a lot about this place," Blair commented as she concentrated on her coffee. She would have preferred to wait, was hoping Nick was an early riser. But Taylor was practically dancing with impatience so she gulped the last of her coffee and rushed after her daughter. There was little chance they would run into him on the mountain—the ski circus was simply too big for such a coincidence. Maybe she would see him before dinner.

"I saw the schedule on the desk last night."

"Since when did you start looking at schedules?" her mother asked.

"Since we spent half an hour waiting for the bus yesterday," came the reply as they reached the door to their room. "Don't worry, Mom." Taylor grinned as she inserted the key. "I didn't look at the map."

Blair chased Taylor into the room, collecting jackets and mittens and other miscellaneous gear. They were dressed for the outdoors in scant minutes, Blair in a stylish mint-green outfit and Taylor in teal blue. They trotted down the steps to the equipment room, changed into ski boots and sorted out their skis and poles from the dozens that were stacked against the walls.

Lumbering along awkwardly in their boots, they just made it to the corner as the bus pulled to a stop. They were the only passengers.

"Are you positive this place is open this early?" Blair asked dubiously.

The early-morning frost on the windows concealed the outside world from them, although Taylor was doing her best to rub through it. "Of course I'm sure," she said, using her fingernail to scrape away the frost.

Blair shuddered at the sound that made, then leaned forward to peer through the circle Taylor had managed to etch on the window. There were people moving around, some of them carrying skis. Reassured, she settled back against the seat.

The gondola that would take them to the top of the mountain was nearly deserted, but it was running, and that was all that counted. Soon they were suspended high overhead, swinging slightly in the light breeze as they traveled upward.

"Can we go there?" Taylor asked, pointing to a deceptively easy run just below them.

"If we can find it," she replied, knowing full well their chances of that were slight. "Let's head for the back side of the mountain first," she suggested, figuring it would be sunny there at this time of the morning, while the slopes below were still shadowed and cold.

"Yeah, *if* we can find it," Taylor kidded.

Blair acknowledged the gibe with a regal nod, affecting a superior air as she tilted her head back and tried to look haughtily down her nose. It was a difficult pose. Her nose wasn't long enough to make the gesture believable. "I'll find it."

"Eventually," Taylor agreed with a grin. "As you've pointed out before, 'There's always tomorrow.'"

Blair grinned, too, then began zipping and buckling and fastening. The top was just ahead.

NICK CHECKED THE MAP against the terrain below him, then thrust it into his pocket and pushed his gloved hands through the loops at the top of his poles. Before moving, he looked uphill for traffic, then shoved off. His movements were precise and controlled, and he paid absolute attention to the challenges in front of him, planning every pole plant, each turn. He was a master of the sport, and enjoyed it more than any other exercise. Moving easily with the ever-changing contour of the hill, Nick cut through the moguls with practiced skill.

He concentrated totally on the hill, never once allowing his thoughts to drift to the woman he'd met last night. He only allowed himself to think of her when he stopped.

Or fell.

From out of nowhere, a streak of green cut across the tips of his skis. He yelled in surprise, then caught an edge as his balance was thrown. A cloud of powder blurred his vision as he tumbled head over heels down the slope, skis and poles flying off in separate directions. He forced himself to go limp, rolling with the hill instead of fighting it.

He was beginning to think he'd never stop. He wondered what idiot had cut in front of him, then wished he'd seen Blair that morning. If he broke his leg, he'd never get the chance to ski with her. Nick spared a few choice words for the green blur that had done this to him as he continued to fall.

His momentum finally ran out, leaving Nick face down in the snow. He lay there quietly, going over a checklist for broken bones and sprains. In between counting whole and healthy limbs, he silently cursed the idiot who had caused the accident. There was no excuse for skiing out of control. At least he *hoped* the other skier had been out of control. He would hate to think they'd done this on purpose! Suddenly the quiet was shattered by a familiar voice.

"Hey, Mom! Great recovery!"

Nick knew that voice! He did a modified push-up, eyes narrowing against the sun as he searched the slope above him. He saw a ski, both poles, then the other ski.

More important, he saw Blair. And his anger turned to excitement.

"That was *not* fun," she said nervously, relieved to see the skier sitting up. It was embarrassing to cause an accident, particularly when she hadn't even fallen herself. At least he wasn't hurt, she thought, noticing he was getting to his feet. He was still too far away for an apology, so she tried to talk sense into her daughter as she moved to retrieve the man's equipment. "It was dangerous. Fast and icy and bumpy and narrow. I don't know why I let you talk me into doing it, you *know* I hate narrow runs! I could have killed someone coming out of the trees so fast."

"He looks okay to me," Taylor said. "Kind of white all over, but he's standing up."

"That's not the point!"

Slipping sideways down the slope to pick up one of her victim's skis, she snuck a look at the man, wondering if he was freezing under all that snow that clung to him. She had the second ski and was sliding across to the poles when Taylor swept past her. Concentrating on balancing the cumbersome load, she didn't realize her daughter had skied down to the man until she heard their voices.

She could be excused for not recognizing Nick under the layers of snow that still covered him, but that voice was unmistakable. She pulled up, taking several deep breaths before she bent over to pick up the poles. She wished it could have been a stranger! Dinner was probably out of the question now.

She'd be lucky if he didn't sue her.

"It wasn't Mom's fault."

"Who're you going to blame it on, then? Peter Rabbit?" he asked, eyes trained on the green ski suit that was slowly coming their way.

Taylor didn't miss a beat. "Would you believe it?"

"Probably not." He took his eyes off the hill and studied the shorter person in front of him. She was a replica of her mother, a miniature version of the woman who'd stolen his dreams last night. The red-blond hair glistened in the sunlight, and Nick was interested to notice her eyes were every bit as expressive as her mother's. She was obviously curious about his reference to Peter Rabbit, yet determined not to ask.

Blair slid across the hill, coming to a smooth stop despite the burden she carried. Dumping the skis on one end, she opened her mouth to apologize, but the look he was giving her forestalled her speech. Her lips remained parted, forming the words that wouldn't come.

He stared at the two of them, mother and daughter. One an enchanting child, the other an exciting woman. He leveled his gaze on Blair's mouth, wondering how it would feel beneath his, then met her eyes with his own, telling her without words what he was thinking.

Nick watched her blink, then again, the deep-blue eyes clearly startled by his unspoken desire. "Teaching by example?" he chided. Distracted by the warmth of his gaze, the desire he wasn't afraid to show, it took her a moment to change gears. She shivered in the warm sunlight. It was difficult to bring herself back to the snow and the hill and the accident. "I kind of got out of control," she admitted uncomfortably. "Taylor saw this trail and wanted to follow it, and...well, you know."

"Yes," he agreed seriously. "I guess I do."

"Sorry," she offered weakly.

"Sorry you came flying out of the trees or sorry you hit me?" he asked.

"I didn't hit you, Nick."

"You left tracks on my skis," he protested mildly, pointing to the neat slashes across the tips.

"Don't tell me you're one of those who cares more for the tops than the bottoms!"

"Now that's something I've never been accused of before," he murmured, the innuendo for Blair's ears only.

On cue, Blair blushed a deep red. Then she tried to get the conversation back on the slope where it belonged. "I'll be more careful next time."

"I'm counting on it," he said, eyes twinkling.

"I don't think he's mad anymore, Mom," Taylor said. "Who is he?"

"Nick Dalton. And I'm not mad," he said. "Just a little cold."

"I *am* sorry, you know," Blair said softly.

"I know." And when she reached up to brush a clump of snow from his hair, he forgave her. Bending down so she could reach better, he stood quietly as she attempted to dislodge the snow before it began to melt. It was worth the accident, having her touch him. It would be worth ten accidents if she'd just take her gloves off, he thought.

"Mom, Mr. Dalton knows Peter Rabbit."

Her face just inches from his, Blair looked into his eyes and raised her eyebrows, daring him to follow this one. "I didn't realize you'd met."

"We haven't," he said seriously. "Not yet."

"But then how . . . ?" Taylor began, trailing off into silence as she grappled with the puzzle.

"He stayed in the room today," Blair offered. "Taylor thought he might have a cold." Having cleared his hair and face of snow, she was suddenly nervous; even with her gloves on, it seemed so intimate to be touching him. She slid back a few feet and leaned on her poles. It was safer to let him do the rest himself.

"A sensible precaution," Nick agreed, his knowing gaze warming her all over. Then, reaching around to brush the snow from the back of his thighs, he continued. "I might be in the same boat as Peter if I don't have a hot drink. There's a hut just around the corner. Why don't you join me?" he asked casually, fitting his boots into the ski bindings.

"How do you know there's a hut there?" Taylor asked, still mystified by the Peter Rabbit puzzle.

"It's on the map."

"Oh, the map," said Taylor expressively. "That's cheating."

"Cheating?"

Taylor shot her mother a look that spoke volumes, then pushed off in the direction Nick had indicated.

Blair laughed at the bewildered expression on Nick's face, then followed in her daughter's wake.

"WHAT DO YOU MEAN, you don't use a map?"

Blair shrugged, more intent on finding the sandwiches in her pack than explaining. Somehow she didn't think Nick would understand.

"It's more fun that way," Taylor piped up. "We just start in the morning and keep going until we're tired."

"How do you know where you are?"

"We don't, not usually.."

"Don't you ever get lost?"

"Yes."

"How do you know where to ski?"

"All slopes go down. . . ."

"Want to split a sandwich?" Blair offered quickly, knowing her daughter could keep up her side of the debate for hours.

Nick didn't answer, but took the half he was offered and hungrily bit off a corner. He chewed slowly, grateful for the excuse to quit talking. He hated losing an argument to an eleven-year-old.

The hot drinks Nick had purchased in the hut combined with the brilliant sunshine to warm them. Blair shed her parka and leaned back against the picnic table, blissfully sunning her face. She knew Nick was watching her, could feel the weight of his gaze.

But Taylor was her safety net. Nick couldn't do or say anything with her daughter hanging on every word. Not really.

"What about dinner tonight?" he asked softly.

She thought about it. She couldn't very well leave Taylor, could she? Then again, it was what her daughter had been pestering her to do for months. So she thought about it some more, was *still* thinking about it when her daughter took over.

Taylor had good ears. And in the end, it wasn't Blair's decision at all.

"Dinner? We had pizza last night," she announced proudly. "Can you top that?"

Blair groaned aloud, keeping her eyes closed and face to the sun. Trust Taylor to assume the invitation included them both.

"They're serving Wiener schnitzel at the hotel tonight," a deep voice said. "I thought we might all eat together."

"And Peter?"

"He's welcome, of course," Nick said blandly. "But he shares *your* dessert, not mine."

"Deal."

"Don't I get to vote on this?" Blair asked, a little miffed that Nick was circumventing the system.

"Depends."

"On what?"

"You only get to vote if the answer is yes. Right, Taylor?"

"Absolutely, Nick."

"That's Mr. Dalton to you, sweetcakes," her mother firmly suggested.

"Mr. Dalton?" Nick and Taylor chorused in unison. Sharing a look of distaste, they simultaneously expanded the thought. "Ugh!"

"What's wrong with Nick?" he asked, challenging Blair to argue.

"Or Uncle Nick?" Taylor tried, remembering her school chum's mother's friend.

Blair cringed.

"Or Mr. D?" he suggested.

"Mr. D?" Taylor repeated, obviously not thrilled by the prospect.

"How about Chester?" Nick threw in.

"Chester?" This time it was mother and daughter who made up the chorus. "Who's Chester?"

Nick grinned. "Me. Nick is my middle name."

"Or Uncle Chester!" Taylor burbled, delighting in the game.

"Enough!" Blair said. "I guess Nick is okay," she conceded. *Anything* was better than Uncle Chester!

Round One to the grinning duo across the table. Blair closed her eyes and lifted her face to the sun. She couldn't stand to see the smug expressions of the winning team.

Uncle Chester? Blair smiled, then laughed out loud. Chester Nicholas Dalton. She was surprised he'd had the nerve to tell them about his first name at all, much less suggest they use it. For a workaholic, he had a decent sense of humor.

Make that suspected workaholic, she instructed herself. Perhaps she'd underestimated Nick. She laughed again.

"SKI WITH ME this afternoon?"

"Sure you can keep up?" Blair challenged, bending to adjust the tension on her boot buckle.

"Let's just say I'd feel better knowing where you are," he drawled. "The same goes for that daughter of yours. She's lightning on the slopes."

"You noticed?"

"I noticed. If she'd had any money, lunch would have been on the table long before *we* finally arrived at the hut," he commented dryly.

"I thought you might be shaky after your fall, so I took it easy," Blair allowed, daring him to challenge her. "A slow run once in a while doesn't bother me."

Nick chuckled, then checked to see that Taylor was occupied exchanging snowballs with some nearby children before he cupped Blair's chin in his palm. "Don't throw dares at me, honey. I *always* win."

"I'll bet you're nothing without your map," she returned, fighting the urge to melt into the arousing warmth of his fingers. It was seductive, being this close to Nick. Exciting. She watched his face, admired the flashing eyes that were alight with laughter. There was a faint mole at the tip of his eyebrow, she noticed, and she wanted to touch it.

"What's the wager?"

Blair licked her lips, drawing Nick's attention to her mouth. It was hard to talk then, even harder to think. "I'll bet lunch tomorrow that we get back to the hotel—before dinner—without using a map."

"That's no bet. I've been here nearly a week. I could find my way back easily."

"Uh-uh. We let Taylor lead."

"That's suicidal!"

"That's fun!" she countered, knowing her daughter *never* missed a meal.

Nick thought about it, then agreed. "But you pay the taxi if we end up on the other side of Austria. Deal?"

"Deal."

And he sealed it with a kiss.

She allowed her eyelids to drift closed when she realized why he was bending over her, drew her tongue along her lips to ready them. This was what she'd dreamed about last night, what she wanted.

He touched her lips lightly, his open mouth tracing their shape as he learned her texture. She stiffened slightly, waiting impatiently for the hard pressure of his lips, the moist warmth of his mouth.

She wanted it all.

And, finally, he gave it to her. Threading his fingers through the long curls at the back of her neck, he held her still as his tongue invaded and plundered and pleasured. She moved with him, opening her mouth wider, inviting him to share the excitement he had created.

Drawing her tongue along the length of his, she explored for herself, delighting in the openness of his response.

"Hey, Mom!"

It was over. The kiss, and whatever else had been happening in those scant moments. Reality was back, and Blair wasn't quite ready to face it. Instead she stumbled away from Nick, disregarding the gentle amusement she saw in his eyes. And the promise. *That* was unmistakable. Snapping her boots into the bindings, she gathered her wits and threw out a reckless challenge to the man and girl who were busy getting themselves set.

"Let's ski!" And she was off, a green blur streaking down the hill.

Nick waited only long enough for the pint-sized blue blur to give chase before he locked his own skis into a matching flight path.

It never occured to him to question his sanity. *That* had flown out the window the first moment he'd laid eyes on Blair. How else could he explain telling her his first name? He'd never shared that secret with anyone!

3

"IT MUST BE fifteen miles back to Kirchberg."

"How do you figure that?" Blair asked with interest. Looking around her, she couldn't see anything that would give her a clue where they were. The flat, narrow ski run was deserted, although she couldn't understand why. It was like a magical wonderland, shaded by tall, snow-covered trees that dripped blobs of the white stuff from their branches on the unwary.

Blair had been hit five or six times, and was presently shaking the most recent bombardment from her hair. Nearby she could hear the noisy babbling of a small stream, the same one they'd crisscrossed on their way down the slope. The man-made bridges that spanned the narrow brook were as much fun to negotiate as the path itself, with its exciting combination of powder and ice—the result of occasional shafts of sunshine that warmed the snow before the shadows smoothed it over with an icy finish.

"I know that because we've been skiing forever, and mostly in the same direction. We must have covered twenty miles of slopes since lunch," Nick said, watching Blair shake the snow from her hair. They were all skiing hatless, the warmth of the early-spring day making cold weather gear unnecessary. Following her down the slopes, Nick had thoroughly enjoyed watching her hair fly wildly in the breeze. It took on a life of its own, and none of Blair's attempts to tame it seemed to work.

But it didn't matter, because it was glorious that way—full of sun and wind and, now, snow. He wanted to touch it, feel its silky texture, bury his face in the soft waves. But he held himself apart from her, letting her deal with the last of the snow by herself.

It was safer that way. No telling what would happen if he gave in to himself. And Taylor was a very effective chaperon, Nick thought ruefully, chuckling under his breath as he pushed off to follow Blair.

"Complaining, Nick?" Blair threw over her shoulder. But she said it with a smile, assured he was only acting the part of a grouch. She'd been watching him all afternoon, and there was no way he could hide his enjoyment of the day's sport.

"Just pointing out that your daughter might possibly have made a wrong turn a few miles back," he retorted.

"Nonsense! Taylor would never make a mistake like that," Blair replied with confidence. "Not with dinnertime so close!"

Nick wished he could cross his fingers, but the thick ski gloves prohibited that. There was no way he had the energy to retrace their path back up the hill, so with a resigned sigh, he kept his skis on a downward heading.

Taylor had taken the lead from her mother before they'd finished the first hill, and her hit-and-miss technique of choosing slopes and lifts had challenged his stamina—not to mention his energy level. They hadn't stopped all afternoon!

Both Taylor and Blair were excellent skiers, and Nick wondered how an eleven-year-old had learned so much in such a short time. She was a natural, though.

Watching her disappear ahead of them down the trail, he admired her casual approach to the unknown.

"Why don't you let me get out the map?" he said. "It's getting late."

"That's the third time you've asked that today," Blair pointed out. "Don't you trust us?"

"No." But he didn't reach for the map.

She laughed, delighted with the teasing manner that had been part of his approach to her all afternoon. He treated Taylor the same way, with one important exception.

He didn't gaze at Taylor with the same hot look in his eyes. As he was doing now . . . communicating without talking, holding her gaze with an intensity that thrilled her.

"I'll bet you're just hungry," she said, hoping the deliberate double entendre would precipitate another kiss. It had been hours since the last one, and she wanted more.

"*Taylor's* hungry. *I'm* just lost."

For a moment, she was disappointed he'd let that one go by, but a quick look at the twinkle in his eyes told her he hadn't missed the invitation. He was just postponing his acceptance.

"Your map won't do you any good." Blair sighed, willing the tension inside her to subside.

"Why not?"

"This slope obviously isn't on a map. If it were, there would be skiers all over it," she pointed out logically. "Aren't we lucky!"

He looked as if he might disagree, but instead chose not to comment at all. They were skiing side by side, slowly gliding down the track in the direction Taylor had disappeared. Rounding a corner, they were suddenly faced with a fork in the trail.

"That way," Blair said, pointing to the right.

"How do you know?" he asked, puzzled by her certainty. Looking at the snow, Nick couldn't distinguish Taylor's tracks from any of the others that had passed this way before them.

"Can't you smell it?" she asked.

"Smell what . . . ?" Then he inhaled, and he understood. "Apple pie?"

"No. Apple strudel. We're in Austria, remember?" Laughing at the resigned expression on his face, she dug her poles into the snow and headed for the source of the tantalizing aroma.

Taylor had found a hut. She was already leaning her skis against the rough-hewn wall of the small restaurant when Blair and Nick finally skidded to a stop. "Come on, Mom! I'm starved!"

"Go on in and order, Taylor," Blair suggested, stepping out of her own skis. "But remember, there's Wiener schnitzel for supper, so don't get carried away."

"You don't really think we'll make it back in time, do you?" Nick asked as he relieved Blair of her skis and leaned them against the wall beside his own. "We don't even know where we are, much less how to get out of here."

"It's only a little after four, Nick. We have loads of time for details." Pulling off her gloves, she thrust her hand through the crook in his arm and gently urged him in the direction of the door. "Come on, now. I'll buy you a *jaegertee*."

"As long as I'm not driving . . ."

"HAVE YOU FIGURED OUT where we are yet?" Nick asked, cupping the warm mug in his palms. Not that he particularly cared, but it would be nice to know, just in case they ever found the energy to leave. He doubted that, because Taylor looked as though she might be napping in the corner of the booth. He didn't blame her. Two cups of hot chocolate and a generous serving of strudel would put anyone out for a while.

Blair, however, didn't look at all fazed by the potent *jaegertee* she'd consumed. Nick groaned silently, determined not to let her hear the exhaustion he was trying so desperately to hide. Taylor's—and, therefore, Blair's—madcap approach to skiing was wearing, particularly as they hadn't seen fit to stop all afternoon. Nick wasn't a stranger to exercise, but it disconcerted him to keep going, slope after slope, skirting heavy traffic by skiing the rugged fall line instead of waiting for it to pass, never making allowances for difficulty. They just charged full-speed ahead, daring the hill to spoil their enjoyment.

No, he'd never had quite that carefree approach. He was still uncomfortable about ignoring maps and guideposts.

In the meantime, it wouldn't do to let Blair know how tired he was, not when she appeared ready to tackle another twenty miles. He wondered how on earth she did it.

"We're in Jochberg."

"Jochberg," he repeated, visualizing the map. Then his eyes widened as he realized where Jochberg fit into the scheme of things. "But that's on the other side of Kitzbühel."

"Actually we're just a tad outside of Jochberg itself," she explained. "The bartender says not a lot of people come through here. Usually just the local crowd, in fact. I can't believe you've been here a week and haven't found this place," Blair commented, forking the last piece of strudel into her mouth as she looked around, admiring the hand-carved wood shelves adorning the cozy room before returning her gaze to the man across the table. "The food is marvelous!"

"It's not on the map."

"See why we don't use one?" she enthused. "There are so many nice surprises like this, especially when you don't tie yourself to a particular route or schedule."

"I passed through Jochberg the other day," he said gruffly, feeling as though he was defending his honor. "The ski safari follows a course through the village," he explained, referring to the cross-country route that allowed skiers to travel from Kirchberg to Pass Thurn, a tiny village at the upper end of the ski circus.

"Then you realize we're not that far away," she said brightly, draining the last of the warm brew. "The bartender says all we have to do is ski down that way a mile or so." She waved her fingers in the general direction. "We'll run into the main road and we can catch the ski bus from there back to the hotel. If we hurry, we'll have time for a sauna before dinner!"

The thought of another mile on skis was his undoing. Nick groaned, aloud this time. He refused to look at Blair, her laughter ringing in his ears. Savoring the last of the *jaegertee*, he continued to ignore her. He studied the empty mug, debating the merits of a refill.

"Tired?" she asked mischievously.

"Who me?" he responded, capturing her eyes with a challenging stare. "I'm not tired. I'm hungry." And then, because Taylor still appeared to be napping, he added softly. "I can't imagine ever being too tired for you."

Was it only last night they'd met? she wondered, the thrill of his frankly sensual gaze freezing her movements. Was this what people were talking about when they referred to the "chemistry" between a man and a woman?

And was "chemistry" enough? Blair couldn't answer that, not now. Catching her breath as he lifted his hand to her face, she sat spellbound, waiting for his touch. When it finally came, it took her heart by surprise, throwing the normally steady beat into an erratic rhythm. He drew a single finger across her cheek, passing lightly over the bridge of her nose as he traced the high cheekbones. Her entire body seemed focused on the path of his fingertip, the trail of fire that ignited separate, far distant fires inside her.

Just a touch, and she was with him. And his kiss had been devastating. She wished he'd do it again. Now.

"Can I have another piece of strudel?" The gentle finger dropped away as Nick leaned back, out of touching distance.

"Of course not, Taylor." Blair took a deep breath, drawing her tongue along dry lips as she sought to erect a facade of normalcy. But it was hard, especially with Nick watching her mouth so earnestly. After a long moment, he shuddered, very slightly. But she'd seen it, had almost felt it.

It was thrilling to know she could do that to him, almost as exciting as the sensations he caused in her. Putting aside for a moment her suspicion that Nick was a workaholic, she wondered if she dared explore the attraction.

She wondered if she had a choice.

In the meantime, there was Taylor. "If we get moving now, we'll get you back to the hotel before you starve to death. Think you can live that long?" she teased, ignoring the smug look of satisfaction in her daughter's eyes. They'd have a talk about that later.

Taylor *never* took naps.

Nick watched them stand and begin to collect their gear. He didn't move. He didn't think he could. Maybe he'd just order another *jaegertee* and hang around here for a while. Looking around the cozy room, he wondered how late they stayed open . . . and if they had a spare bed.

"Come on, Chester," Blair teased, reaching over to poke his side with a punishing finger. "We can't leave you here. You'll never get back without us. Remember, it's not on the map."

"Yeah, Chester. Mom's right," Taylor joined in. "And if we hurry, you can have that sauna Mom was talking about." The young girl squealed and scooted out of the booth as Nick made a grab for her.

The midget hadn't been asleep after all.

"CAN I TRY the sauna tomorrow?" Taylor asked her mother.

"That's 'May I,' " Blair corrected absently, more concerned with checking the table for any food that might have been overlooked. Except for the crust of bread on Nick's plate, there wasn't any. She wondered if the pizza place delivered.

"*May* I try the sauna tomorrow?" Taylor asked, rolling her eyes at the correction. Nick chuckled, then shut up quickly when Blair glared at him.

"I suppose so, if we get back sooner," she said, then asked Nick if he was going to eat his crust.

"Still hungry, Blair?" he asked mildly, studying her empty plate before lifting his eyes to tease hers.

His amusement at her appetite should have been embarrassing, but she ignored it and took the crust. "You only had to ski with Taylor half a day. I've been at it since eight this morning. Besides, you ate half my sandwich." She signaled the waitress for more bread.

"Can I stay up late tonight?"

"How late?" Blair asked automatically, lavishly spreading butter on the crust.

"Just until I finish my book. I've only got a couple of chapters left."

"I guess that's okay," she decided. "But not too late. We need to get an early start tomorrow if you want those new boots."

"New boots?" Nick asked.

"Yeah," Taylor said enthusiastically. "The old ones are scrunching my toes."

"They didn't seem to bother you until you saw that hot-looking turquoise pair in the shop," Blair said.

"Well, they *are* terrific, don't you think?"

"*I* think they'll clash with your ski outfit," Blair countered, immediately regretting her words.

"Speaking of my ski outfit...." Taylor began, but her mother didn't let her complete the sentence.

"I guess turquoise and teal blue won't be so bad together," Blair said.

"But, Mom..."

"And Peter agrees with me. Don't you, Peter?" she asked, addressing the blue-coated rabbit perched on the corner of the table alongside the sugar and salt. After an appropriate pause, Blair aimed a challenging stare at her daughter. "See, Taylor? Peter agrees. Teal and turquoise are 'in.'"

"So what does *he* know about fashion?" Taylor shot a malevolent glare at the offending cottontail.

"Unless you've decided against the boots?" Blair asked innocently, concentrating on the basket of bread the waitress deposited in front of her. Pumpernickel. She hated pumpernickel. With a sigh, Blair decided she wasn't *that* hungry, and pushed the bread basket aside.

Taylor stared at her mother, then prudently decided she'd pushed far enough. "I guess they'll be okay. Do you think the store opens early?"

"I guarantee it," she said dryly. They wouldn't miss an opportunity like that, she knew. Ski resorts were big business, and the expense of it all sometimes made her dizzy. Not that she couldn't afford it, but it was a consideration nonetheless. How would Taylor ever learn the value of anything if there were no limits?

Nick watched the ease with which Blair enforced her decision, marveling at the skill involved. It wasn't easy to say no to kids, he knew. His sister had four children, and sometimes complained that her vocabulary was reduced to a single, negative word.

He wondered how Blair had managed to raise Taylor alone, or if she had. There hadn't been a chance to talk all day, not even on the chair lifts. They had made it a point to double up with Taylor, neither of them comfortable about leaving her to share the double chair with a stranger. As a result, he knew practically nothing about either of them.

But he knew enough to want to know more. A lot more.

With only one day's skiing left, that didn't leave him much time.

Looking around the room he saw several families playing cards or board games on the dinner table. There wasn't much else for kids to do at a ski resort, unless they went for a toboggan ride in the moonlight, which

Nick didn't even consider. Straightening in his chair, he challenged them to a game of gin rummy.

"Gin rummy?" Taylor asked disbelievingly, leaning back so the waitress could clear their table. "Why not poker?"

"Because if I lose, you won't get your new boots tomorrow," Blair interjected firmly. "Gin isn't nearly as expensive." Then, just to be on the safe side, she set the limits at one groschen a point—about one-tenth of an American penny. She wasn't taking any chances.

Taylor grumbled under her breath as Nick pulled a pack of cards out of a breast pocket. Blair watched his long fingers as he shuffled and dealt the cards, fascinated by his easy movements.

They played for an hour, Blair losing steadily to Taylor and Nick before she called an end to the slaughter. "What happened to the days when you let me win?" she quizzed her daughter, mildly embarrassed by her inability to take any points whatsoever.

"That's hearts, Mom," Taylor reminded her. "I *never* let you win gin rummy."

"Where did you learn to play cards, midget?" Nick asked, relieved Blair had ended the game. Staying even with Taylor hadn't been easy going. He'd even begun to suspect Peter was helping her on the sly.

"Monte Carlo," she replied with a straight face, ruining the effect by lapsing into a giggle when she saw the look of disbelief on Nick's face.

Nick grinned, and decided to tease the girl a little. "If you've played Monte Carlo, you must be good. So why didn't you win enough to pay for your new boots?"

That sent Taylor into another fit of the giggles, and Blair shook her head in exasperation. "Don't be silly. Taylor's too young to gamble."

"No!" he exclaimed, pretending shock.

"Aw, Mom!" Taylor protested. "You blew it!"

Blair shot her daughter a firm glance. "We don't need to give the impression that we lead a wild life, Taylor." It was unusual enough, she thought silently, without adding elements such as gambling. To Nick, she explained with a minimum of fuss. "We rented an apartment from a man who dealt blackjack at one of the casinos. He got a kick out of teaching Taylor a few things." She didn't mention that Taylor was pretty good at blackjack. That wasn't something a mother bragged about.

"That could be dangerous," Nick finally said, leaving the rest of his questions for later, when Taylor was in bed. But at least he now understood how the friendly game of cards had turned into a cutthroat contest. Well . . . at least Taylor had provided him with a challenge. Blair didn't seem to have the knack for gin.

"Now you see why I didn't want to play poker!" Blair joked. She'd have to explain, she knew. About Monte Carlo, for a start. But maybe that could come later. For now, she didn't want to spoil anything by getting down to facts. It was okay just *suspecting* their life-styles were totally, completely opposed to each other.

Knowing the truth was another matter. Knowing would change everything.

SHE HADN'T SAID she'd be back.

Nick waited anyway, nursing the beer he'd ordered after Blair had dragged a reluctant Taylor off to bed. Letting his gaze drift along the length of the bar, he watched the scene with a sense of detachment. Nothing was different from the previous night. The same crowd of people talked and drank and laughed, sharing in the party spirit as they rhapsodized over their day's adventures. There had been a few nights when Nick had joined them. But last night, he'd been too busy watching Blair.

And tonight, he just waited for her to return.

He checked his watch, again. And when he looked up, she was there. He watched as she made her way slowly across the room, slipping into the gaps between skiers with an expertise he admired. Nick took pleasure in watching her, appreciating the tight fit of the jeans she wore with a soft, deep-blue sweater. She looked even better than he'd imagined last night, now that she'd discarded the bulky after-ski gear for something much more flattering.

He'd spent most of dinner trying not to stare at her. With Taylor there, it was important to stay cool and collected. But now, with the young girl tucked into her bed, he could let Blair know he appreciated what he was seeing. When she finally arrived at the table, he stood slowly, dragging his gaze upward. His eyes lingered for a long moment on the gentle swell of her breasts before coming to rest on her mouth. And then, after a long, hard stare at her parted lips, he met her gaze.

"I've been wanting to kiss you all night. But I think I'll wait a little longer," he said slowly. "I might not be able to stop . . . once I touch you."

Blair gulped. The hot, hungry stare had already fired her senses, his words only added to the flames. Somehow she hadn't expected this. He'd been so cool during dinner, laughing with Taylor, teasing them both, she'd almost forgotten that wildness he could make her feel with his look, his touch.

He could do with one look what no man had ever accomplished with the most ardent caress. Blair didn't understand that, was even vaguely disturbed by it. Perhaps it was simply her imagination, she thought, then knew better when she focused again on his frankly sensual stare.

"What's the coat for?" he asked, pointing at the parka she carried under one arm. She wouldn't need a coat where he wanted to take her. His room was already warm, and he would make her warmer still, would make her hot with his kisses, with his touch. Hot, wild, exciting. She would be everything he imagined, everything his body demanded.

He'd only kissed her once, but still he knew.

Blair took a deep breath, then shuddered when his gaze fell to enjoy the slight movement of her breasts. She needed air, lots of it. "I...I thought I'd go for a walk" she stammered, then clenched her teeth against the chills that were zipping up and down her spine. She shook out the parka and pulled it on, hiding her eyes from his probing gaze as she stuffed the walkie-talkie into a pocket. It was too intense, she told herself. She couldn't handle this sudden flood of sensations.

She hardly knew him.

Nick watched her for a moment. He had an idea why she was avoiding looking at him, mostly because this uncontrolled rush of excitement was also new to him. He'd been attracted to women before. Excited by them, passionate with them.

But he'd never wanted a woman as much as he wanted Blair. It scared him, as he believed it scared her.

"Can you wait for me to get a coat?" he asked. If she said no, he'd go without one. Coat or no coat, he wasn't letting her walk away from him.

She nodded, then jerked her head up as he threaded his fingers through hers. "Don't hide from me, Blair. It's not fair."

And then, seeing the silent agreement, he led her out of the bar and into the lobby. He didn't like leaving her there, but he knew if he took her along to his room, he might not be able to stop himself from taking what he wanted.

Nick didn't like feeling out of control.

"HOW LONG were you in Monte Carlo?"

"About ten months," she replied, cautiously stepping over the pile of snow that had drifted onto the sidewalk. The path was slippery, and she was grateful when Nick pulled her gloved hand through the crook of his elbow. Blair felt safe then, even safer when she curled her other hand into the thick padding of his jacket. If she took a spill on the treacherous ice, she wouldn't go down alone.

"And since then?" he probed, liking the feel of her snuggled into his side.

She shrugged with one shoulder, making light of their travels as she listed the places they'd visited. "We spent some time in Portugal, then France. We've been in Bruges since August. Wasn't the snow perfect today!" she enthused, trying to change the subject. Questions about where she lived would inevitably lead to more about what she did. And then there would be comparisons, and finally, the realization that they had nothing whatsoever in common.

No, she really didn't want to get into it.

"Bruges," he repeated, ignoring her reference to the snow conditions. "But that's in Belgium."

He was determined to know it all. Blair sighed, then decided that as long as she was going to learn the truth about him, she might as well get it over.

"Tell me, Nick," she said, ignoring the curiosity he couldn't mask. "Where do *you* live?"

"New Jersey," he said. "Why?"

"Humor me," she urged, pulling him to a stop at the edge of the path. "Why do you live in New Jersey?"

"Because my work is there."

"Of course it is," she commented, the depression that was encroaching an almost physical sensation. "Let me guess," she insisted, hoping against hope she was wrong. "You're an executive in a large company."

"Almost," he admitted, searching her moonlit face for a clue as to where this discussion was headed. "It's my company."

Blair sighed heavily, closing her eyes against the frustration of being right. It was even worse than she'd expected, he *owned* the company.

"How often do you go on vacation?"

He shrugged, mentally tallying the holidays he'd skipped over the years before admitting, "Usually once a year to ski. Sometimes I take a weekend off to see some friends, but things have been busy since I started the company."

"And when was that?"

"About twelve years ago," he said, surprising himself more than her. Had it really been that long?

She nodded, his answers confirming everything she'd already dreaded. A man wasn't successful by dabbling at business. He had to be consumed by it, live his work as if that were all there was to life. And nobody knew that better than she did.

"Blair, what's this all about?"

She ignored his impatience, carefully studying features barely visible in the shadows. "I'd guess you're about thirty-six, maybe thirty-seven," she mused aloud, then raised an eyebrow to indicate this, too, was a question.

"Thirty-eight."

Blair nodded, satisfied she had enough facts to support her case. "Nick, you're a thirty-eight-year-old workaholic."

"But . . ."

"Don't argue, Nick. You can't hide it from me," she said, wagging a cautioning finger in front of his nose. "I recognize the symptoms. You see, *I* used to be one!"

4

"*YOU* WERE A thirty-eight-year-old workaholic?"

"No!" Grabbing his wrists for balance, she struggled to keep from losing her temper, not to mention her footing. The ice beneath her feet threatened to undermine her dignity, but the real threat was Nick's teasing response to her accusation. He didn't understand, and Blair wasn't sure how far she was willing to go to rectify that.

"You were married to one?" he suggested.

"No! No! No!" she shouted in frustration. "I'm thirty-two, not thirty-eight!"

"Trust a woman to get touchy about her age," he chided, gently massaging her shoulders through the thick down parka.

Blair squeezed her eyes shut tight against the comfort he was offering. She had to get through to him, make him understand. "I was a workaholic," she admitted solemnly, then opened her eyes and said it again. "I was a workaholic. For nine years, the focus of my life was my job."

There was a silence then, a long one. Blair held his questioning gaze, the cleansing effects of admitting her past sins leaving her weak and chilled. The silence surrounded them, the unbroken quiet of the empty street magnifying the moment. She watched him in the moonlight, knew he was finally hearing her, could see the confusion that crossed his face. She almost ran then, mortified by her outburst, wishing the frozen ground would somehow open up and swallow her. What was very real and traumatic to her must appear melodramatic to Nick, but that hadn't stopped her from trying to make him understand.

Nick took the only option open to him. Lifting his hands from her shoulders, he eased his wrists from her grasp and slid his fingers into her hair. He filled his hands with the soft, silky curls, holding her quiet for his kiss.

She was startled at first, then forgot why as he sidetracked her thoughts with his mouth. His lips covered hers lightly, warming her with their gentleness. She shivered as the chill inside was replaced with something very tender. It was new to her, this almost fragile emotion he was creating. She luxuriated in the feeling, soft sounds of contentment escaping her lips as she opened herself up for more.

Only the feeling changed then. He spread his fingers to cup the back of her head, and it was a different kind of warmth that surged through her. This was hotter, more exciting. His mouth demanded more than gentleness now. Blair slid her hands up the satiny front of his parka, grabbing handfuls of the bulky material when he invaded her mouth. He took her lips and parted them with little patience, plunging his tongue inside with hungry stabs that touched every nerve.

Her knees quivered and threatened to collapse, but still he didn't stop. Instead Nick wrapped a single arm tightly around her waist, holding her firmly against his body as he coaxed her tongue into an erotic dance. She followed his lead easily, chasing his teasing tongue back and forth, learning the exciting textures of his mouth, the smooth chill of his teeth. He captured her tongue, sucking lightly before chasing her away with a strong thrust.

She clung to him, he held her close. It was a sharing that was so basic—so *right*—she was incapable of pulling away. The heat was intense, the night forgotten.

"Mom!" The disembodied voice sliced between them, pushing them apart with a suddenness that was totally disorienting. "Mom! My stomach hurts!"

Nick dropped his hold on her, stunned by the interruption. Heedless of the ice, Blair jumped backward and promptly lost her footing. With the grace of an elephant on skates, she flailed briefly and dropped into an ungainly mass of arms and legs.

"Ouch!" she muttered aloud while running silently through an entire list of words that should not have been part of her vocabulary. But she was used to disciplining her mouth around Taylor, and it was habit that made her keep the unladylike expressions unspoken.

"Ouch?" Nick asked as he reached down to pull her upright. "That's it?" he asked suspiciously, leaning close to eavesdrop on what she was saying under her breath.

Blair smiled insincerely, then bit her tongue. Not that it mattered that she could cuss as fluently as a sailor, but somehow she thought the knowledge would give Nick something else to snicker about. It was enough that he was brushing the snow from her bottom!

Suddenly remembering Taylor, Blair pulled out the walkie-talkie, relieved to hear her daughter's voice respond. It would have been too embarrassing to have broken the silly thing on the ice!

"So what's this about a stomachache, kiddo?" she asked, unsuccessfully trying to ignore the hands that still brushed at her snow-covered thighs.

"Can I take some of that pink stuff, Mom? I think I ate something bad."

"Wait until I get there, Taylor," Blair instructed, reaching around to thrust her fingers into Nick's hair. Once they were firmly anchored, she pulled steadily until he was standing beside her. Relieved to have his hands off her legs, she shot him a quelling no-nonsense look that at once chastised him for his overzealous efforts to clean off the snow and let him know how much those "innocent" hands had disturbed her. "You know better than to take medicine without me."

Nick was totally unabashed, grinning at her from a moderately safe distance of about two feet. But he waited obediently, warming his hands in the deep pockets of his parka.

"Okay, Mom. See you in a minute."

Blair thrust the receiver into her pocket and turned back to the hotel, relieved when once again Nick drew her hand through the crook of his arm. Her tush certainly didn't need another bruising, not today. Besides, it was comforting, and she just plain liked walking with him.

"Will you meet me in the bar after you see Taylor?" he asked, pushing open the door to the lodge. "I think we've got a few things to talk about." He drew her around to face him.

"I don't think so, Nick. Not tonight." She was afraid to come back, uncomfortable with the wild response he'd coaxed from her just moments ago. It had never been like that before, never that wild, never that out of control. She'd forgotten everyone and everything except Nick.

And now, in the security of the hotel lobby, he frightened her. Not because he could make her feel new and wonderful things. No, Nick frightened her because when he left, he'd take those new feelings with him.

Blair didn't think she wanted to feel that loss . . . that pain.

"Ski with me tomorrow?" he asked.

"We have to go shopping for those boots," she said. "No telling how long that'll take. I wouldn't want to make you wait on us." She looked away from his gaze and busied herself stamping loose snow from her boots.

"I wouldn't mind."

"I know. But I would."

"Tomorrow is my last day," he said quietly.

She'd been wrong about the pain. It was already there, undeniable and incredibly strong. But she blocked it from her heart, and pretended a lack of concern she didn't feel.

"That's a shame, Nick. You must hate to leave all this lovely snow. Unless it's snowing in New Jersey...?" she asked offhandedly, turning toward the stairs. She needed to get out of there. Now, before he discovered her silly reaction.

It had been a kiss, just a kiss. Blair had been embarrassed by her own melodramatic confession earlier, but she knew this would be worse. Letting him see how much she didn't want him to leave would probably surprise Nick, even amuse him.

"No, not New Jersey," he said from just behind her, startling Blair with the realization that he'd followed her. "I've got a conference in Erice."

"Erice?" Blair stopped on the stairs, turning to face him as she tried to solve the geographical puzzle in her head. "Erice . . . Italy?"

"It's actually on Sicily. But last I heard, Sicily was still part of Italy," he answered, then swatted her bottom to get her moving again. "I'll probably be there a week or so. Now don't you think Taylor's waited long enough?"

"Yeah. Taylor," she remembered, chagrined by the time she'd taken to respond to her daughter's call. Stomachaches weren't emergencies, though, and Blair was having a few problems of her own . . . such as trying to remember Nick was from New Jersey and she'd never see him again after tomorrow.

They arrived at her door, and she inserted the key. But Nick stopped her from turning the handle, lifting her chin with a single finger to capture her eyes. "I'll ski without you tomorrow if I have to," he said gruffly. "But I won't like it. Try to catch up if you can," he dared, knowing the challenge might entice her more than any other technique. "If you haven't caught me by the end of the day, I'll just wait for you in the sauna."

"But . . ." she protested, knowing the odds of finding him in the enormous ski area were against her.

"But nothing, Blair," he said firmly, backing away a few steps down the hall. "I want to see you tomorrow. And I won't like it if I have to wait all day."

He left her then, a smile almost touching her lips as she watched him stride down the hall and down the stairs. A challenge, she thought. A dare.

Perhaps that mountain wasn't so big after all, she mused. And if they skied really fast . . . A dare. She liked it! Pushing open the door to their room, Blair knew she'd take him up on it.

One look at Taylor and Blair knew she was the victim of a false alarm. Snuggled comfortably into an overstuffed chair near the window, Taylor looked anything but sick.

"So what's up, Taylor?" Blair asked suspiciously, deftly removing the half-eaten banana from her daughter's fingers before checking her forehead for signs of a fever. There was none, just as she'd suspected.

Totally unrepentant, Taylor pointed out the window and said, "I thought things might be getting out of control. That's all."

Blair studied the view, finding without much difficulty the exact spot where she and Nick had been standing earlier. In the revealing light of a full moon, Taylor would have missed very little of the scene below. She blushed to think her daughter had been watching the intimate moment, then remembered Taylor was nearly a teenager. Besides, it had only been a kiss . . . nothing more.

"You shouldn't have been watching, Taylor," she said, thinking if she could make her daughter defensive, she wouldn't pursue it. It didn't work.

"Mom, if you didn't want me to watch, you shouldn't have kissed him in front of my window!" she pointed out logically, reaching for the banana that Blair held just out of her grasp.

"I didn't kiss him. He kissed me."

"Not from where I was watching!" Taylor teased, giving up on the banana and settling for pretzels. Tearing the box open, she rummaged inside for a moment before coming out with a handful.

Blair suddenly realized what Taylor was about to stuff into her mouth and grabbed the box, thrusting the girl's hand back inside until she let go of the pretzels. "You're supposed to have a stomachache!"

"Nope. I just thought things might be getting out of hand, so I faked the stomachache in case you needed to bail out. Face it, Mom, you haven't exactly had a lot of experience lately with men."

"And what gave you the right to make my decisions for me?" she asked, holding the pretzels and banana just out of reach. "I'm supposed to be the adult around here, remember?"

"You're out of practice, Mom. I just wanted to give you an out. That's all." Jumping to her feet, Taylor headed across the room. "Now you can meet him in the bar or whatever if you want. But you can always keep the stomachache excuse if that's what feels right."

"You're entirely too old for your age," Blair said darkly. But it was hard to criticize, especially in an age when children were exposed to sex education in grade school. And she'd always encouraged the mature streak in Taylor, somehow hoping a factual approach to life would serve to protect her from the dangers of being a child in today's world.

Blair followed Taylor to the refrigerator, slamming the door before the young girl could decide what she wanted. "You *will* have a stomachache if you don't stop eating. Besides, it's time we were both in bed." And after a hard look that dared Taylor to say anything more about what she'd interrupted, Blair snagged her nightgown from the closet and huffed her way into the bathroom.

Another night like tonight, and her dignity would be in shreds! Blair went through the steps of preparing for bed, blithely avoiding thinking about anything more than tomorrow's challenge. Several minutes later, she returned to the bedroom and found Taylor in bed, buried under the covers with not a hair in sight. Probably avoiding a lecture about interfering, Blair thought, grateful her daughter had chosen the chicken's way out. She wasn't up to a debate, not about Nick.

They'd need an early start, she decided, setting the alarm for an almost painful hour. She flicked off the light and snuggled under the cold sheets, shivering for endless minutes before the trend reversed and her body warmth returned.

Her last thoughts before sleep were on the dare. Their only chance would be to catch him before he got too far. Perhaps they'd give the boots a miss, and trail him when he left for the slopes.

It would only be cheating if he caught them, she ruled drowsily.

THE DOUBLE BLUR caught him by surprise.

Even though he'd been halfway looking over his shoulder all morning, they'd still managed to catch him unawares. Flashing out of the trees, they intercepted him on the verge of a particularly tricky bit of the mountain, one cutting above and the other below as they zoomed past him down the slope.

It was a good thing he was standing still.

Before his eyes, the daring duo slashed back and forth across the hill, making child's play out of the field of moguls. They were laughing with each other, and probably at him, he thought ruefully as he put some power behind his poles and shoved off his perch at the crest. If he let them get their way, they'd most likely be waiting for him at the bottom of the hill, lounging around in that special way they had that told him they'd been waiting for hours.

They weren't going to get away with it.

Catching up with Taylor and Blair wasn't easy, and passing was probably the most foolish thing he'd ever attempted. But he did it, making a special point of showering each in a cloud of powder as he plunged down the slope.

All he got for his efforts was a delighted giggle from Taylor and a four-letter word from her mother when he cut her off and sent her flying toward the trees. But she recovered faster than he would have liked, and he'd barely pulled up to a stop at the bottom of the chair lift when the pair skidded up beside him.

"Great skiing, Nick! When did *you* get so brave?" Taylor teased, reaching down to unbuckle the top of her boot, drawing his attention to the new equipment.

He ignored the gibe. After all, he'd won the impromptu race, hadn't he? "Love the boots, midget. But can't they go any faster?"

"You'll see fast, buster! I was just taking your age into consideration," she joked. "Next run you might not get so lucky."

Nick laughed outright, and pushed Taylor into the snow: "Enough sass out of you, midget." Taylor was just getting ready to retaliate with a handful of snow whan Blair intervened.

"Hit *me* with that and you can find your own lunch," she threatened, digging her poles into the snow with mock seriousness. Taylor's gaze darted from her mother, to Nick to the rapidly disintegrating handful of snow. Taylor made the right decision, although she fooled no one with her meek acceptance of the situation. Blair and Nick exchanged warning glances, then picked the girl up by the armpits and slid over to join the lift line.

"There's a ski hut near the top," Nick said, pushing Taylor slightly ahead and then resting an arm around Blair's shoulders to keep her at his side. "If we have an early lunch, we'll beat the crowd." And give his legs a rest, he thought, his knees just a bit shaky after that last run.

Blair eyed him suspiciously, but kept her thoughts to herself. It wasn't Nick's fault he tired easily. Besides, she liked the feel of his arm around her. "Do we have to ski with a map this afternoon?" she asked, having spent the entire morning following the precise trail he'd traced on the ski map she'd found at their breakfast table.

"It wasn't so bad, Mom," Taylor pointed out. She twisted as far around as her boots would permit, letting her eyes rest on the pair behind her. A glance told Nick she hadn't missed anything, and her smile told him she didn't care if she had. "If he hadn't left the map, we might not have caught up for another hour or so," she bragged, daring Nick to disagree.

Blair sighed, not quite sure Taylor wasn't right. They'd been skiing so fast it was a miracle they hadn't caught up with him earlier. Maybe they'd take it easy now, she hoped. Her legs were just a little unsteady.

"Lunch sounds great," she enthused. "We've got sandwiches, but some soup would taste good." Under her breath, she added, "A *jaegertee* wouldn't go amiss, either."

Waiting for their turn, they shared adventure stories, Blair and Taylor making fun of each other's disasters, Nick listening in bemused silence. The only excitement he'd had that morning was falling off the T-bar drag lift almost before he'd gotten started, and he didn't feel much like sharing that.

Finally they were at the head of the lift line, and Blair and Taylor boarded the next chair while Nick shared with a heavy-built, German-speaking matron who kept saying "good ski, ja?" and "skinny blonde make good wife." Nick didn't attempt to do more than add his own series of "ski good, ja!" and "blond daughter a handful."

Blair and Taylor didn't get the joke when the woman skied off the chair at the top of the hill and shook her fist at Taylor, saying "mind you papa," before skiing off down the hill. Nick composed his features, the resulting expression a combination of innocence and wicked humor.

"'Mind you papa?'" Blair asked incredulously.

"'Mind you papa?'" Taylor repeated, lifting an eyebrow in exact imitation of her mother. "Flirting with an older woman, Nick?" she asked, following the trail of the Austrian matron with her eyes.

"That's Uncle Nick to you, squirt," he said blandly. "And we were just discussing the weather."

"Sure you were!" And Taylor headed across the slope to the hut, too hungry to tease Nick anymore. That could wait for later.

When Blair didn't move to follow, Nick tried to end the issue. "Can I help it if she doesn't know you can't get pregnant by kissing?" Grinning wickedly, he turned to follow Taylor before Blair could hit him.

"*What! What did you tell her?*" Blair screamed at his back, then pushed off the mogul in an endeavor to catch up. But the effort was doomed, mainly because she'd forgotten to put her hands through the loops on her poles, and they stayed right where she'd been standing. Tracking back up the hill, Blair fumed and fussed and simmered, and didn't actually start laughing until she'd reached the poles. She was still chuckling when she finally caught up with Taylor and Nick who were enjoying a close-range snowball fight. She ducked instinctively as they turned their aim on her, screaming vague threats about lunch and dinner and breakfast for the next week. They might not have understood the words, but they got the gist of her intent, because the barrage of snow suddenly stopped.

Blair led the way inside and settled for a cold beer and hot soup, toasting Taylor's hot chocolate and Nick's mulled wine as he set fire to both maps—the one he carried and the one he'd left on their breakfast table. The small blaze invited the attention of their host, but Nick used his broken German to explain.

"Map kaput."

"Map kaput?" the man repeated, somewhat mollified the fire was contained to the ashtray. "Was ist los?" he added, going totally over their heads with his native command of the language.

Blair and Taylor fell off the bench in a fit of giggles, leaving a rather chagrined Nick to explain. But he couldn't, mostly because the tears in his eyes were fogging his concentration. So he just mumbled something that sounded like "ski good, ja?" before his forehead fell weakly against the tablecloth.

Shaking his head, the host walked away. Nick didn't see him leave, just prayed he would. Surreptitiously wiping the tears of laughter from his eyes, he watched as Blair and Taylor picked themselves up and scooted back onto the bench.

"Map kaput?" Blair repeated, going off into another peal of laughter. Still laughing, she and Taylor collected their gear and followed Nick outside. It took longer than usual to get the buckles locked and zippers zipped, mostly because they weren't trying very hard. Nick had just about had enough of Blair's ribbing when Taylor threw him a personal challenge.

"So you think these boots are all show and no speed," she said, eyeing the competition with a mean look. "Well, buster, eat my dust!" And she swooped down the slope, flying fast and low.

Blair and Nick exchanged looks, then chorused, "Eat my dust?"

And the race was on.

"But that sign means the slope is closed." Nick looked warily over the rise, noting the tracks of a mere handful of skiers disappearing down the hill.

"No, it doesn't. It just means it's not groomed," Taylor argued. "And he said it went right to the hotel," she said, referring to a man they'd talked with in the lift line.

The sign they were arguing about had a single word—'*VERBOTEN*'—with a red slash across it. Nick wished he hadn't burned the map. There were translations on the back page for situations like these.

Taylor finally noticed the tracks. "See, Nick. We're not the only ones who've skied it. And just think of the advantages," she persisted. "We'll end up at the hotel. No walking. No waiting for a bus."

"Maybe not, honey..." Blair began, a sinking feeling in the pit of her stomach giving her second thoughts about the expedition.

"Aw, come on, Mom!" Taylor begged. "You always say we need to try new things! That run we skied yesterday wasn't on the map and it was terrific. And this one's even got a name," she said, pointing to the marker off to the side. "It's got to be okay," she finished with faultless logic.

"Well, I guess . . ."

Taylor didn't let her mother finish. Squealing her delight, she dug in her poles and headed across the easy slope.

"I still think this is a rotten idea," Nick said darkly, shooting Blair a resentful glance. "We'll probably get killed." And he was getting too tired for the challenge of an ungroomed slope. The sun was just dropping behind the mountain, making the going tough with flat light and long afternoon shadows.

"Don't be a spoilsport, Nick," Blair said easily. "The worst that can happen is they'll take away our lift passes. And what do you care? You're leaving tomorrow!"

Still, he hurried to keep up with them, sensing a need to get this over with before something went wrong. They stayed with the trail of the skiers who had passed this way before, taking it slow for a change. Then Nick passed Taylor and Blair, getting the rhythm of the crusty snow and enjoying the easy pace.

He didn't see the fence until it was too late, but he yelled anyway, hoping to divert Blair and Taylor. The loop of barbed wire slipped around his ski, grabbed his boot and whipped him over the ledge head first.

"*Nick!*" He heard the scream as he tumbled through the sky, knew he'd recognize Blair's voice anywhere. Then he crashed into the side of the mountain, his foot still entangled in the barbed wire.

It was a miracle that he stopped. Nick breathed deeply, then opened his eyes. He was alive, and a brief survey provided a bright spot of information. His limbs were still whole.

"You're upside down, Nick."

Taylor came into focus as she expertly skied past the hazard and down into the gully. Her boots were at eye level, and Nick had a good chance to admire them. Turquoise. He'd never joke about them again.

"You okay?' Taylor asked, crouching down to look at him eye to eye.

"Yeah," he managed. "But I think I'm stuck."

"Mom's working on that," Taylor offered, stepping out of her own skis at her mother's order.

"The wire's caught on your boot," Blair shouted, still trembling with fright. "You sure you're okay?"

"Are my skis all right?" he asked instead. They were new, and he liked them a lot. Even with the slice marks Blair left on their otherwise perfect tops, he liked them.

"You must be okay if you're worried about your bloody skis," Blair muttered, then backed off a little to study his predicament. "The wire is all the way around. We'll have to take off your boot."

"Take off my boot and I'll fall on my face," Nick pointed out. It was only a foot or so down, but he wasn't in the mood to be dropped on his head.

"You got any better ideas?" Blair asked with just a touch of irritation.

"Your face is turning awful red, Nick," Taylor noticed.

"Try to keep him from landing too hard, Taylor. I'm going to pop the buckles," Blair decided, then leaned forward to do it before Nick could argue.

Nick heard first one snap, then the second, and gravity took over. He tumbled into Taylor's arms, sweeping the girl beneath him as his body came crashing down into the gully.

"Gosh, you're heavy," she grunted, then stuck a boot into his back as she scooted free. "You really should be more careful, Nick," she suggested, prudently staying out of range as he straightened into a sitting position.

"I *knew* this slope was a rotten idea," he muttered, catching the boot that Blair had managed to untangle.

"Seems like I'm always picking up after you, Nick," she sighed, easing down the slope with his skis in hand.

"Maybe you shouldn't go so fast, Nick," Taylor suggested kindly. "We'll wait for you. Won't we, Mom?" she asked Blair, a solemn expression on her face.

"Maybe you shouldn't go so fast," he mimicked, snapping his boot closed with unnecessary force. But the sarcasm was lost on Blair and Taylor. They were too busy laughing to pay him any attention.

They were still laughing when he stepped into his skis, and he fed their merriment with his next warning. "Now stay behind me and *go slow!*"

"Don't you want me to lead?" Taylor threw a glance at the barbed wire that Nick had secured around a nearby post.

"I said stay behind me and I meant it," he huffed, hiding behind a gruff front to conceal his worry. The last thing they needed was a real accident.

"Yes, Taylor," Blair agreed. "Mind you papa."

And they collapsed on another wave of laughter, this time taking Nick with them.

5

It was so hot Nick could almost feel his bones melt into the wooden slats of the bench. He didn't care, could barely think. He considered lying down, then rejected the thought. Changing positions was too much work.

Then there was the sound of the sauna's door opening, bringing with it a gust of fresh air and familiar voices.

"See, Mom, I told you he'd be hiding in here."

Through slitted lids, he watched Taylor climb onto the top bench opposite, concentrating on her so as not to look at her mother. He didn't think he could stand knowing if she looked as good in a bathing suit as he imagined. Not with the midget watching.

"It's impossible to hide in a sauna," Nick pointed out. "There's nowhere to go."

"If the steam was really thick . . ." Taylor suggested, then made a move toward the water bucket.

"It's thick enough," he said, effectively stopping the girl from throwing more water on the hot stones. Any hotter and he'd never walk again. Taylor shrugged and returned to the top bench, muttering something like spoilsport under her breath. Nick heard her, but ignored it. Just being alive made him feel magnanimous.

"He's not hiding," Blair said reasonably. "He knew we were coming." Blair seated herself on a low bench, still clutching the towel she'd brought with her. "Didn't you, Nick?"

"Mmmmm."

It was more a growl than an answer, and Blair stole a glance at him... the first real look in his direction since they'd entered the sauna. He was sitting propped up against the paneled wall, one leg slightly bent at the knee, the other flat on the bench.

He was magnificent. He was stunning.

He was naked.

Blair gasped, her eyes widening as she double-checked her discovery, her gaze darting to the area shielded from view by his slightly raised thigh and forearm. The slight noise caught Nick's attention, and his body shifted as he turned in her direction. She shivered, incapable of looking away, her thoughts bouncing between his nudity and Taylor's presence and her own reaction. Her eyes were glazed, nervous anticipation coupling with dread as his legs and arm moved to reveal... swimming trunks.

She was incredibly relieved to focus on a strip of nylon that decently covered everything that should be covered. She tried not to think about the niggling disappointment that her discovery had produced.

Dragging her gaze from the suit, she forced herself to meet Nick's eyes. A swift glance at his amused expression was enough to make Blair look elsewhere. She studied the ceiling, checked out the nonexistent decor of the plain room and watched as her daughter succumbed to the heat. Taylor lay down on the bench, pillowed her head in her arms and shut her eyes.

Blair didn't surrender to the steamy allure of the sauna. There was a heat from within that quickened her heartbeat. She knew he was watching her, could feel the weight of his gaze through the light cloud of steam that rose steadily from the stones. She tried to ignore him, just to see if she could do it.

She couldn't. Her body responded to his gaze with a sensual tightening that was becoming a familiar by-product of Nick's presence. The towel she clutched fell away as her lifeless fingers lost their grasp.

And finally she raised her eyes to meet his.

He had waited for her, not moving. The amusement was gone. In its place was a hot, hungry stare that raked her body with little regard for time and place. She stiffened, drawing her arms tightly around herself before she remembered.

She'd done the same thing to him. And he was inviting her to do it again. It was there, in his eyes. A dare to look, to see what he was, the body that held the soul. It wasn't a game, but a demand to give her eyes pleasure, just as he was enjoying the view from his perspective.

Watching without touching. It was a sense of the forbidden that made Blair drop her arms and open herself to his gaze.

There was so much of Nick exposed to view it was almost overwhelming. His broad shoulders were smooth, glistening with sweat. Her fingers itched to touch, knowing the muscles there would be tight and hard. His arms and chest were lightly covered with fair hair, as were his legs, but it was more dense there. Blair was fascinated by the beads of sweat that worked their way down his chest toward the narrowing arrow of hair on his stomach, leaving wet, slick trails on his belly.

Blair heard him cough, watched the rippling of muscles as the slight spasm shook his body. But he coughed again, and this time the patently fake noise got her at-

tention. Guilty eyes flew to meet his accusing stare, and
she meekly removed her gaze.

"Enough is enough," he suggested quietly, then
dragged a white hotel towel over his lap, ignoring the
startled giggle from Blair.

The exchange had taken mere seconds, less than a
minute, but he was more aroused then he'd been in his
entire life. Looking at Blair...having her eyes on him....

Blair couldn't help snickering again.

"Mom, it's too hot in here."

"It's supposed to be hot in here, Taylor," Blair said
reasonably, then dragged the towel back to her shoulders. "But you're right," she agreed. "It's *too* hot. I'm
getting out." Much too hot, she thought silently with
an unexpected shiver.

"You've been here about three minutes," Nick
pointed out, daring Blair to stay. But his heart wasn't
in it. Having her that close, almost naked, and in a place
that wasn't private... No, it was too dangerous. No
telling what might happen.

He could wait.

Blair stood on shaky legs and cracked open the door
before looking over her shoulder at Taylor, studiously
avoiding the other side of the room where Nick sat
quietly. "Coming?"

"Sure." Taylor galloped down the benches to join her
mother.

Nick roused himself enough to make sure they'd have
dinner with him.

When the door closed behind them, he leaned into
the wall, willing his body to forget the hot flames Blair
had ignited. He couldn't leave the sauna, not until the
physical evidence of his arousal eased.

He hoped he wouldn't melt in the meantime.

"WHY BRUGES?"

"Because we like it there."

"And Monte Carlo?" he persisted, determined to get some answers. Last night Blair had dodged the questions, using his job and life-style to avoid answering him. But tonight was his last chance to learn more about her.

Unless he somehow managed to see her again . . .

He'd been thinking about it in the sauna. For that matter, the subject of Blair and Taylor had rarely left his thoughts since he'd met them. He was interested in Blair, very interested. Logically he understood the attraction. She was a striking woman, full of life and easy to be with. He enjoyed her wit and admired her energy.

The other part, the chemistry between them, was neither logical nor something he could control. It was exciting just to be near her, and common sense had nothing to do with it.

He wanted her. And he had the uncomfortable feeling that one night with Blair would never be enough.

Which brought him back to the questions of Bruges and Monte Carlo. How could he ever catch a gypsy, much less keep up with one? It made sense to find these things out now, before he became too involved . . . Before logic was superceded by emotion.

Secretly Nick feared it was already too late.

Blair sighed, then reached for the carafe of red wine the waitress had brought with their meal. The food was gone now, as was Taylor. She was alone with Nick, sharing with him the silence of the empty dining room. They'd elected to remain at the table rather then move to the bar after Taylor had departed for bed. Now she

wished there was a little noise to cloak the sudden tension in the room.

He was a stranger, she reminded herself. But the
kisses they'd shared hadn't been those of strangers.

"What's wrong with Monte Carlo?" she finally
asked, taking a long sip from the glass. She avoided his
eyes, studying instead the tablecloth, the wine she
swirled with nervous fingers . . . anything but Nick.

"Nothing, I suppose," he said slowly. "I just can't
figure out why you chose it, unless your job took you
there. It just doesn't seem to be an obvious choice,
especially for a kid." That was something else that puzzled him. What did she do for a living that provided
funds for a skiing holiday in Austria. There weren't too
many people that could afford that kind of a life, but
perhaps her family was supporting them. Somehow,
though, that didn't sound like Blair.

"Besides being none of your business, you know
nothing about it!" Her eyes flashed as she locked on to
his probing gaze. "And who are you to judge how or
where I should raise my daughter?"

"Why are you so defensive about it?" he asked mildly,
a little surprised at her vehemence.

"I'm not defensive!"

"Then why don't you tell me about it?" he suggested
reasonably, allowing his eyes to drift away from the
confrontation in her gaze.

Why not? she asked herself. Because he wouldn't
understand? Or because he wouldn't approve?

And why, she asked herself, *did it matter?*

Nick was leaving tomorrow, would be out of her life
forever. The chances of seeing him again were nil, and
Blair suddenly wanted to make him understand.

"It's simple, really," she began, turning in her chair to face him. "I was exactly what I told you last night— a workaholic. My career consumed me. I was possessed by the need to be working, achieving, promoting and being promoted. My job was everything, it got my undivided attention. And Taylor was the excuse for it all.

"In my mind, I *had* to work hard, to provide for Taylor, to prove to the world that I could do it, and do it alone. If I couldn't give her a father, then I could give her everything else. I thought I was making up for her having only one parent."

"And instead, she had none," Nick said.

"Yes," she admitted. "I missed most of Taylor's childhood, was never home long enough to do more than pay the housekeeper. I hardly saw her, didn't even make the day-to-day decisions that most mothers have to deal with—like what to buy little Roy for his birthday or what to wear to Sandy's party. Or even what to eat and when to eat it.

"She was almost nine before I figured out what a mess I was making of our lives." Blair sipped the wine, reflecting on how stupid she'd been. "It took me nine long years to realize Taylor had no real family, no one she could rely on to be there for her."

"Lots of kids grow up without two parents," he said slowly, recognizing the pain she still felt from those lost years. "It seems to me you did the best you knew how."

"But I know better now," she said, feeling once again the rush of love that Taylor had made possible. "I know that she doesn't need things, she needs me."

"She loves you," he said simply, and covered her trembling fingers with his own.

"She does. That's the best part of it all," she said
softly, her eyes misting as she remembered the first time
Taylor had said the words. "She saved it for me, all
those years when she was lonely and unhappy. She
waited for me, had the faith I'd someday be a real
mother to her."

"Maybe she's always known you love her," he suggested.

"Perhaps. I don't think it's that simple. Nothing is
ever that simple." Blair had often thought about that
part. She wondered how Taylor had known she'd
always loved her, especially when she hadn't realized it
herself.

For the first time, she noticed Nick's hand covering
her own. It was a warm feeling and made her feel secure. What difference could all this make to him? Why
had he even bothered to pursue it? Despite her questions, she didn't doubt his sincerity, not for a moment.

Blair suddenly realized there would be a huge gap in
her life after he left, and wondered how he could have
made such an impression on her in just two days. It
didn't seem possible, but it was true.

"And now that you've left the terrible world of big
business, what do you do for a living?" It seemed like
a safe subject, he thought. Showing an interest in what
she currently did was certain to be less risky than digging into her past.

"Oh, this and that," she said lightly. "When I feel like
it—"

He interrupted, disbelief accenting his words.
"Nothing regular?"

"Not really. Just the odd job every now and then to
keep me out of trouble."

"So how do you and Taylor manage?"

"We get by." And that was the end of *that* subject as far as Blair was concerned. No way would she tell Nick about any of the odd jobs she'd taken over the past couple of years. He was obviously too straitlaced to understand her need to experiment. Her two-week stint renting beach umbrellas would definitely horrify him— and that was mild compared to some of the other jobs she'd taken!

And she wouldn't tell him that money wasn't a problem, either. It somehow rubbed against the grain to have to defend herself.

"As in, it's none of my business?" he finally deduced, finding this topic a little riskier than he'd expected.

She just smiled.

"So what does all of this have to do with Monte Carlo?" he said quietly, drawing her thoughts back to the original question.

"It's not so much about Monte Carlo as it is about New York."

"What's wrong with New York?"

"In general, nothing," she said, dismissing the metropolis with a wave of the hand. "But I wanted a complete change. I thought that if I stayed in New York, I might be tempted to work again. Europe sounded like a wonderful place to live, and I liked the idea of exposing Taylor to different languages and cultures. We talked about it, all during the time when I was selling the house and finishing up my contract. She wanted it too, almost more than I did."

"She would have gone with you to Timbuktu."

"We still might," Blair joked, then wondered exactly where it was. Nothing was impossible, but geography had never been her strong point.

"So which one of you chose Monte Carlo?"

"Taylor. She'd seen a TV movie about Grace Kelly, and thought it sounded like a fairy-tale place to live." Blair smiled at the recollection, remembering her own intial misgivings. It had been an expensive year, particularly with the bilingual school Taylor had attended. But it had been worth it. Taylor was now fluent in French, and they'd made lasting friends. She explained this to Nick, relaxing now that he knew it all and hadn't shown any of the disapproval she had come to expect from others.

"Correct me if I'm wrong, but didn't Grace Kelly live in Monaco—not Monte Carlo?"

Blair nodded, grinning at his mystified expression. "When I bought the plane tickets, I got confused. And by the time we figured out the mistake, we'd already fallen in love with the place." She shrugged, then added, "Geography was never my strong suit."

She told him about her friends from the old days in New York and even her sister—all of whom disapproved. They'd said it wasn't the proper way to bring up a child, that Blair was selfish and dragging Taylor around Europe would eventually harm the child. Blair disagreed, arguing that home was where love was, not a certain place or house.

And they weren't as nomadic as it appeared. She made sure they stayed in a single place for the entire school year, venturing out only during holidays and summer vacations. Blair was happy sharing her life with Taylor, and her daughter loved the excitement of new places and people.

"I can see why you get a touch defensive," he said, drawing his fingers along the length of hers in a motion so slow it captured her attention. "I can even understand why you thought I'd be one of 'them.'"

Blair shivered as she watched the slow movement of his fingers, enjoying the light touch even as she had the grace to blush. "Sorry about that. As much as I'm convinced I'm doing the right thing, I don't deal well with criticism." Suddenly it occurred to her that while he'd listened and understood, he hadn't supported her decision.

"What do you really think about it?" she asked, trying to ignore the steady warmth that was building from his simple caress, "About Taylor and the way we're living. Given the same set of circumstances, would you do the same thing?"

Nick took his time, tracing up one finger and down the next as he thought about his answer. He wanted to tell her yes, that he approved and thought she was doing what was good and right.

But he didn't agree.

It wasn't that he didn't believe Taylor and Blair were a happy family, or that the travel was a good thing for the young girl.

"No, probably not. I still think a child needs a home," he finally said, not surprised when Blair pulled her hand away.

"I give her a home," she said evenly. He hadn't understood after all.

"I meant a stable home. One with a swing in the backyard and a handful of lifelong buddies down the block. A place she can come back to, year after year." It had been his dream, all through his childhood. But his father's military career had made it an impossible dream, moving them from one state to the next, overseas and back again. The constant change had never stopped, and as his father rose higher in rank, the moves had increased in frequency.

But the dream had become something he knew he would give his children—a place to call home.

"Your concept of home is different from mine," she said softly, wishing she'd never asked the question. What did it matter what he thought about her life-style? Even as she had the thought, she knew it mattered a great deal.

"It's certainly more traditional," he agreed.

Everything she'd said in the past hour pointed to the differences between them, and it was with reluctance that he admitted everyone would be better off if he left for Erice tomorrow and never saw Blair again.

But could he stand to leave without knowing her softness, the feel of her beneath him in that ultimate moment of sharing?

"All of this shouldn't matter," she whispered, letting the sensual ache he aroused inside her wash over the disappointment. "Why can't we get past it?"

Nick reached out to take her hand again, insisting on the contact when she was reluctant to comply. He threaded his fingers through hers, holding her troubled gaze as he tried to make sense of it all. Touching her set off the flame, again, and he peered into the seductive darkness of her eyes, sharing his heat and feeding on her excitement.

But still he tried for a commonsense answer. "I think it matters because this thing between us is so strong. You overwhelm me," he murmured. "I've never felt anything like it before."

"It scares me," she admitted softly. "You scare me." And she turned her hand within his, seeking a bond that was elusive and totally impractical. But she didn't draw away. She couldn't.

"Is that why you've been trying to keep our life-styles between us?" he asked gently, knowing the answer, yet wanting to hear the words.

"It'll never work," Blair whispered. "You're everything I left behind."

"And you're everything I don't want," he agreed, then amended the sentence. "Your *life-style* is everything I don't want. But you..." he said, and took a deep breath, "I want you very much." With his other hand, he reached out to touch her face, his finger seeking the curve of her ear. She was sensitive there, he saw, noticing her barely audible gasp as he lightly traced the delicate inner shell, the soft hollow behind it. He wondered how she would react if he put his tongue there, a wet, hard thrust into the center of the shell.

It excited him just thinking about it, and suddenly all the words and reasons and logic didn't matter. He wanted her. She wanted him. The rest was unimportant baggage.

"You're leaving tomorrow," she murmured. "I don't think I could let you go if ..." But her eyes said she would, because tomorrow no longer mattered. She needed him, now. Tonight.

"I don't think I could leave if ..." But he knew he would, because he had to.

"Let's go to your room." She said it quietly, without any sense of wrong or right. It was more a feeling of the inevitable that made her say the words.

His mouth curved into a smile. She had guts, this woman. She knew tomorrow would hurt, but had put that aside for the moment. He wondered which of them would hurt more, knowing his own pain at leaving her would be no small thing.

They didn't belong together, but that didn't seem to matter. They would never meet again, but that was no longer important. Nick threaded his fingers into the heavy curls at her neck, massaging the tense muscles beneath. He didn't kiss her, not yet. He'd lost himself before in the taste of her, knew the sensual power she wielded could make him forget time and place.

Nick smiled again, then let his hand fall away from her hair before rising from his chair. "Let's go," he whispered, pulling her to stand beside him.

They stood there a moment, fingers entwined, otherwise not touching. There didn't seem to be in any hurry, though they both knew their time was limited.

They wanted it to be slow.

Blair wanted to remember every second. Nick knew he'd never forget a moment with her.

"There's an overseas call for you, Mr. Dalton."

The suddenness of the interruption shattered the illusion of privacy, destroying the mood as effectively as a cold shower.

"Take a message," he ground out, physically over-powering Blair's attempt to withdraw her hand. If he could keep touching her, there was still a chance.

"They said it was important," the man persisted.

Nick closed his eyes in frustration, then allowed Blair to slip her hand away. It was gone...the mood, the fragile understanding. He told the man he'd be right there, then turned to Blair.

But she was ready for him, her resistance an almost physical thing between them. "I guess I'll see you at breakfast."

"I won't be there. My transport to the airport leaves before then," he said. "Wait here for me...or in the bar. I won't be long." He tried not to plead. She wouldn't like that.

"I don't think so, Nick." And she moved away, just enough to prevent her fingers from seeking the warmth of his hand.

He didn't argue, because there was nothing left to say.

WALKING AWAY from Nick had been easy. Well, perhaps a little painful, she admitted, but that was just the frustration getting in the way. Otherwise it had been a snap.

Cupping the warm mug of heavily sweetened coffee with both hands, Blair carefully considered just how much she should tell Taylor. She was still thinking about it when the child in question interrupted her thoughts.

"What'cha thinking about, Mom?" she asked between mouthfuls.

"Crete."

"Crete?" Taylor repeated, reaching across her mother's plate for the bread basket.

Blair let the minor misdemeanor get by. Table manners could be discussed another time, when she was in a less cheerful mood. Right now, they had plans to make.

"Yes, Taylor. Crete. The place we were going to when we left here."

"*Were* going?" Taylor was quick to note the promised seaside holiday was no longer a sure thing. "But you promised!"

Blair shook her head. "No. I promised sun and sand. Crete just happened to fit the bill."

"But we've already booked a hotel," Taylor pointed out, still not ready to give up.

Blair waved away that problem with a flick of her wrist. "That's minor. We can always cancel." She took another sip of coffee, then began to lay the foundation for their new destination. "Besides, we don't know anyone on Crete."

"That's never stopped us before," Taylor said, suddenly suspicious of the direction the conversation was headed. "I thought you *liked* it that way."

Blair refused to answer on the grounds she might incriminate herself, then pursued her train of thought. "I was just thinking Erice might be a better choice."

"Erice?" Taylor put down the roll she was buttering and prepared to square off with her mother. "So who do we know in Erice—wherever that is?"

"It's on Sicily, and that's part of Italy last I heard," Blair supplied, then dropped her eyes before Taylor could see the faint flush of embarassment.

"And . . . ?"

"And Nick will be there all week."

"Aha!" Taylor exclaimed, then bit into the roll and spoke over a mouthful of poppy seeds and marmalade. "You're chasing Nick!"

Blair bristled at the accusation, but was incapable of refuting her daughter's conclusion. Still, she tried to present it in a more palatable way. "It's more like we're following him."

"Why?"

"Because he's fun?" Blair checked out Taylor's reaction, then tried again. "Because we like him? *I* like him."

"Okay." Taylor nodded in agreement. "But does Nick know about this?"

"Not really." Blair squirmed under her daughter's gaze, then admitted the whole truth. "He hasn't a clue."

"Boy, will *he* be surprised!" Taylor exclaimed.

Blair just smiled weakly, and crossed her fingers under the table.

6

"BUT I THOUGHT you could speak *some* Italian!"

"French and Flemish, Mom. Not a single word of Italian. We missed that trip to Venice last year 'cause you had to drive the carriage for Frankie."

"Oh. I guess I forgot."

"If we'd gone to Crete like we planned, we wouldn't have this problem."

"But I *know* you can't speak Greek, Taylor."

"True. But we wouldn't be looking for him on Crete. *That's* where the problem is."

"So if we can't get this waiter to understand us, how are we going to find out if he's here? This place is an absolute maze of rooms and cubbyholes."

"I'll flip you for it. The winner gets to distract the waiter while the loser runs through the place screaming for Nick."

They were looking for him.

He hadn't been positive until Taylor had actually said his name. They could have been looking for anyone, he figured. But they wanted him. It was the shock, he guessed, that slowed his reactions. They weren't supposed to be here.

They were still dithering about tactics when he spoke from his table behind the curtained alcove. "I'd check that coin if you know what's good for you, Blair. Sure sounds like a setup to me."

"Bingo!" Taylor cried gleefully, oblivious to the annoyed stares of nearby diners.

Blair gasped in pleasure at the deep rumbling of his voice, then flicked aside the curtain to find Nick seated alone at a table laden with an incredible assortment of food.

She was ashamed to admit the food drew her eyes before the man, but she *was* hungry. This was the fifth restaurant they'd tried, and walking away from the tantalizing aromas of the previous four had finally taken its toll.

But the man ultimately captured her attention. Totally.

It had been four days, an eternity. Nick held her gaze, accepting her presence with the same hungry stare that poured out of her own eyes, filling her soul with a yearning she couldn't control.

Nothing had changed. Not the excitement she felt just being near him, not the tumult he could elicit with only a look. It was real, this wildness she sensed, a shared feeling neither could control.

And they both felt the wanting.

"Hi'ya, Nick," Taylor greeted him, shouldering aside her mother to grab a chair. "Good thing we stopped by. I'd hate to see you get fat trying to eat all that by yourself!"

"There *does* seem to be a lot here," he admitted, dragging his gaze from Blair. The erotic slant of his thoughts was harder to check, but he made a valiant effort. There would be time for that later.

Blair was here. Totally unexpected, absolutely welcome.

He concentrated on the subject of food. "I think the problem with the quantity here is my Italian, not my appetite, midget."

Blair edged closer to the table and finally sank into an empty chair. "Hope you weren't expecting anyone, Nick," she ventured before snagging a shrimp from a nearby platter. Holding it by its fantail, she drew the succulent meat into her mouth and, with a calculated bite, severed the edible part from the bit between her fingers.

"No guests," he confirmed, following the delicate movements of her tongue and lips. "Can I at least get you a plate?"

"With your luck, we'd end up with raw oysters and chopsticks," Taylor scoffed. "Let me try."

"I thought you didn't speak Italian," Blair objected, studying the antipasto in front of Nick before reaching over to pilfer a pimento-stuffed olive.

"I don't. But French is the language of food," she reminded the adults with just the right amount of superiority in her tone. "It's worth a shot."

"So why didn't you try French before?" Blair asked around the olive in her mouth.

"I guess I wasn't hungry enough."

Nick listened with interest as Taylor ran a string of melodic phrases past the hovering waiter. He wasn't really surprised when the Italian responded with a similar—but shorter—set of words. With a condescending smile at Nick and Blair and a deferential nod at Taylor, the waiter turned and sped off on his mission.

"Did you understand as much of that as I did?" he asked Blair, trying hard not to stare as she delicately licked excess sauce from the tip of her finger.

"Less, I think," she said, finishing one finger and starting on the next.

"I'd feel a whole lot better if you used a napkin," he suggested quietly, swallowing hard to contain the surge of hot desire her simple act had provoked.

Blair looked up in surprise, and found herself confronted with the astonishing knowledge that they didn't even have to touch each other to feel the tension. It was between them, always, an almost physical presence.

The hard part was trying to act as if it wasn't there at all.

Fortunately, an eleven-year-old could cut through the atmosphere with just a word or a look . . . and not even realize she was doing it!

"Yeah, Mom," Taylor joined in. "Don't be a slob. How will I ever learn anything if you set such a poor example?"

"I don't have a napkin," she pointed out. "What do you want me to do—wipe my fingers on my slacks?"

"Yes." No doubt about it, Nick thought. Slacks could be cleaned, but the erotic picture of Blair licking her fingers had nearly stretched his nerves to the breaking point!

"If Taylor could learn French, why not you?" he asked, rapping her lightly on the knuckles with his fork as she reached for a wedge of tomato. "And if you want a tomato, have Taylor order you one," he added with just a hint of threat in his voice. "That one's mine."

"Oh." Philosophically, she gave up the tomato and popped another shrimp into her mouth. A balanced diet wasn't everything.

"What about the French?" he prodded, relieved when the curtain opened to reveal the waiter with the necessary eating equipment. With mild trepidation, he lis-

tened as Taylor opened negotiations with the waiter,
hoping he had enough cash to cover whatever she was
ordering. He hadn't planned on sponsoring a buffet for
the hungry hordes, and plastic wasn't popular in small
restaurants like this. Before he could interrupt to ask,
Blair answered his question.

"I tried to learn French, but quickly figured out that
I'm incapable of speaking through my nose."

Nick nodded, understanding perfectly. His ability
with the language was just as limited. "You're lousy at
cards and languages—not to mention geography—and
can't be trusted with a stuffed animal," he summarized
in a tone that was meant to irritate her. "So what *can*
you do?"

"I can outski you any day, buster," she said sternly.
"Pick your mountain."

"I'd say that's a chicken's dare, considering the,
er...lack of opportunity." And he passed the shrimp
to Taylor before Blair could finish off the platter.

"I'm just as good on water," Blair bragged, shooting
a glance at Taylor that dared her to differ.

The waiter returned, interrupting all conversation
with a tray loaded with an assortment of exotic-looking
dishes. With a little shifting and consolidating, he ar-
ranged everything on the table and left them with a
murmured phrase that Taylor translated as "enjoy your
meal." Considering the overwhelming amount of food
on the table, Blair figured he'd really said "good luck,"
but was unable to convince anyone else.

"Fast service around here," Blair commented, wondering how the food had been delivered so quickly as
she dug in to the pasta dish beside her.

"I asked him to bring stuff they already had prepared," Taylor admitted, tearing off an enormous

chunk of bread before passing the basket to Nick. "And I told him you hadn't fed me in ages. I think he felt sorry for me."

Blair thought she could stand the embarrassment, particularly since Taylor's tactics had gotten the necessary results.

"Think we can eat all of this?" Nick asked no one in particular.

Neither Blair nor Taylor bothered to answer. They were too busy eating. In self-defense, he followed their example.

They didn't eat it all, but the few scraps that were left wouldn't have satisfied a snacking gerbil. Blair watched as her daughter drank the rest of her milk, then shifted her gaze to Nick. He, too, was watching Taylor.

"How many days did you say it's been since your last meal?" Nick joked, reaching over to poke Taylor in the ribs.

She giggled, then poked him back, laughing harder when he grunted under her assault. "We missed lunch 'cause the plane was late and the bus from Palermo took decades. Then we just decided to wait until we found you."

Blair just groaned and wished she'd worn a skirt with an elastic waistband.

The waiter returned to clear off the table, the admiration in his eyes unmistakable. After pouring the remaining wine into the two glasses, he mumbled something to Taylor which produced a violent shake of her head.

"What did he say?" Nick asked after he'd left.

"He asked what we wanted for dessert," Taylor moaned.

"I would have decked him," Blair said tersely, sneaking a finger under her waistband in an attempt to relieve the pressure.

He'd missed them. Nick felt the surge of pleasure and identified the source as Blair and Taylor. Letting his eyes drift from Blair to Taylor and back again, he acknowledged it. Since leaving Austria, his days had been dull and boring.

They had turned a simple meal into an event. It was exciting just being near them. Nothing like the excitement Blair created inside him—that was something altogether different. But taken separately or as a pair, mother and daughter, they made him feel alive.

But they were supposed to be on Crete, not in Erice. It was time to ask the question.

"I've been wondering what you're doing here," he said, leaning back against the cushions of his chair. He tried not to look too concerned, studying the wineglass as if it were made of the finest crystal and deserved his full attention.

"Eating." Blair beat Taylor to the answer, a killing glance at Taylor defying her to say otherwise.

"Besides that," Nick prodded, hoping Taylor wouldn't be intimidated by her mother. He hadn't missed the quelling stare.

"I'd tell you, but Mom would blush...just before she killed me," Taylor said innocently, her wide-eyed look daring her mother to find fault with her answer.

"An idea not without merit," Blair muttered as she avoided looking in Nick's direction. "Children should be seen and not heard."

"Without this child we wouldn't have gotten plates and napkins," Taylor reminded her practically. But the waiter arrived before either adult could argue, and Nick and Blair debated for several moments over the bill. The money was finally in the waiter's pocket when Taylor suddenly decided she had to "go," and she went off in search of the bathroom, leaving Nick and Blair alone in the secluded alcove.

He didn't waste any time.

"I need to know why you're here." He wanted the words, needed to lay down a clear outline. Just guessing or hoping wasn't good enough. He needed to *know*. Holding her gaze with gentle strength of will, he asked for honesty between them.

"I promised Taylor sun and sand," she said. "Unfortunately you didn't warn me Erice was perched on top of a two-thousand-five-hundred-foot mountain."

He nodded, waiting for the rest.

"And I needed to see you again." There! It was out. Never had she managed such candor with a man. But then, never had anything seemed so important. For that matter, she'd never chased any other man across Europe just for the opportunity to know him better. Hesitantly, when she saw he wasn't going to throw her words in her face, she added, "I thought we left some things up in the air when you left Kirchberg."

He nodded again, then lifted his hand from the table to reach for hers. Carefully studying the contrast of his fingers as they mingled with hers, he said softly, just loud enough for her ears, "You're a brave woman, Blair Forrest. Incredibly brave."

And beautiful he added silently. In the light of a single candle, she looked more beautiful than ever, yet he couldn't put his finger on the reason for it. Her eyes sparkled, apprehension and plain nervous energy vying for dominance in their depths. Her hair was the same wind-blown mess he'd come to expect from her, probably more so than usual although he wouldn't swear to it. He couldn't imagine it tamed into a rigid style...that wouldn't be Blair's way.

Nothing about her was tame.

"Anyone else would say I was a brazen hussy for chasing you down here." She wove her fingers through his, seeking to share his warmth. "Are you sure you don't think that?"

He smiled with just the corner of his mouth, eclipsing her fears with an ease that comforted her. "You spent the two days we were together pointing out how little we have in common, putting distance between us at every opportunity. And still you came." He shook his head slowly as if he were truly amazed. "I think it doesn't matter as much as you would like to believe."

Blair had nothing to say to that. She'd gone with her instincts and had ended up doing the right thing. At least, she hoped it was the right thing. Time would tell, she knew. She'd done her part. Now, it seemed, the rest was up to fate.

"I'm glad you came," he murmured, clasping her hand tightly in an effort to convince her.

"You really don't mind?"

"Do I *look* like I mind?" he asked, the deep pitch of his voice sending chills up her spine.

Blair had to look at him to answer that, even though she'd already guessed what she would see. But, not for the first time, she was wrong.

She thought she'd see desire, the sensual hunger he'd trained her to expect. Instead she saw his pleasure, and she basked in the welcoming glow of his smile as his warmth curled through her.

It was new, this thing he was making her feel. Blair wasn't sure how or why she sensed the difference, but it was there, deep inside. She held his gaze, intuitively masking the newborn awareness as she reflected on what it meant.

She was attracted to Nick, she knew that. More than attracted, she admitted. She was fascinated by him. And it wasn't just a physical thing—sex, she corrected herself, hoping the jolt of the three-letter word might knock some sense into her head.

It didn't work. Sex, making love, sharing a passion—nothing seemed to dim the gentle warmth she felt just having him near. No, she decided, it wasn't just sex. It couldn't be.

It was more.

Blair knew herself well enough to realize that sex—however powerful the promise might be—was not sufficient to have drawn her halfway across Europe.

Yes, it was more. But knowing that much was just the beginning, and she carefully stopped herself from jumping to any conclusions. So she smiled back at Nick, holding his gaze even when she felt the draft of the curtain being opened behind her.

"Hey, Mom," Taylor burbled, flopping gracelessly into her chair, "they've got a *fountain* in there!"

"In where?" Blair asked absently, reluctantly slipping her hand from Nick's grasp. She reached instead for the empty wineglass, finding this new texture a striking disappointment after the rough warmth of Nick's hand.

"In the courtyard by the bathroom, of course," Taylor said crossly. "Can I have a quarter to throw into it?"

"May I," Blair automatically corrected, then dug into her wallet for a coin. She pulled out one, then studied it closely before tossing it back and taking another.

"And what happened to the days when a person could throw a penny into the well and still get their wish?"

"I haven't been alive that long, Mom," Taylor said matter-of-factly. "The farthest back I can remember is dimes. You must be talking of the olden days."

"Cheeky kid you've got there," Nick commented, pulling a coin out of his pocket and handing it to Taylor. Blair was still checking the contents of her wallet, studying each coin one by one. Apparently she wasn't one of those who believed travel was easier if you separated the coinage of different countries!

"Thanks, Nick," Taylor said as she dashed back through the curtain.

"Yes, Nick. Thanks." Blair gratefully put her wallet back into her purse.

"WHAT'S IT LIKE staying in a monastery, Nick?"

"It's not really a monastery, midget," he said, pulling Blair's hand through the crook in his arm as they strolled along the narrow cobblestoned street. The shops were all closed now, and with the hotels at the lower end of the town, there were very few tourists left prowling the misty night. The smooth stones were slick with a veil of moisture, and Nick used this excuse to pull her closer to his side. "It used to be one, but now it's kind of a conference center, a place where they have classes or meetings for whoever wants to book the place."

Taylor nodded in understanding, apparently disillusioned that Nick wasn't rubbing elbows with berobed monks and brothers of the faith. "Too bad," she said aloud. "I'd've liked to see you in one of those costumes with the spooky hood and sleeves that are big enough to hold your lunch *and* your dinner!"

"All you ever think about is food," Blair chastised her daughter. "Besides, it's not a costume, it's more like a cloak," she said. "But you're right, Taylor. I'll bet Nick is smashing in a skirt!"

Nick shot her a look that promised revenge, then abruptly changed the subject. "How did you know where to find me?"

"Easy. You said you were attending a conference, and the monastery is Erice's only meeting center."

"Lucky for you," he breathed. Enjoying the night and the walk and the feel of her beside him, he watched as Taylor skipped a few yards ahead to turn down a steep dark alley with a single miserly light at the other end. "If this meeting had been in Rome, it wouldn't have been so easy."

"If it had been in Rome, I doubt if I could have persuaded Taylor to come," Blair admitted, thankful she hadn't had to face that obstacle. "Frankly, finding you at the restaurant was the hard part. I was beginning to think we'd never catch up."

"But there are dozens of restaurants here," he protested. "How did you manage to find me so easily?"

"Elementary, Watson," she said, tapping the side of her head to suggest the complex workings of her brain. "The monastery—excuse me, the conference center. They gave us the same list they gave you. We just started at the top."

"That list still has ten or twelve restaurants. Were you planning to go to all of them?" he asked, finding it hard to believe she'd go to that much effort. But then, hadn't Blair just come all the way from Austria to be with him? The thought stirred his senses, and he wished suddenly for the privacy of his room . . . any room!

"Who's Watson, Mom?"

"He did some work with Sherlock Holmes, honey," Blair said vaguely, then answered Nick's question. "We found you on the fifth try. I figure we were good for one more restaurant, maybe two, before the need for food got in the way."

She didn't dare look at him. He knew why she'd come to Erice, more or less. At least he knew part of it.

But he didn't know it all. And for that matter, Blair admitted neither did she.

"Where are you staying?" Nick asked suddenly. The fog was beginning to thicken, and he thought it better to get them back to their hotel before he lost his sense of direction.

"Down that street about a block, then left." Blair pointed the way, although it was unnecessary. Taylor was in the lead, as usual, and doing quite well without any direction from her mother. "It's a friend's house."

"Why didn't you bring your friend to dinner?" he asked, curious as to why they'd ventured out on their own, especially their first night in town. He didn't even particularly care if the friend was male. If the friend was a "he," then he was just that—a friend. Nick was beginning to know Blair, and knew without asking that she didn't play those kinds of games.

"I guess he left yesterday for Paris," she said. "When I called to beg an invitation, he said something about meeting Cinda after her show was over. I think this time he's going to marry her," Blair confided, not at all concerned that Nick was barely following the conversation. "But Frederico's housekeeper said we could stay as long as we wanted. At least, that's what I *think* she said. Her English is kind of marginal."

"Hey, Nick." Taylor had already reached the front gate and looked ready to disappear inside. "We're going to the beach tomorrow. Can you come?"

"Afraid not, midget," he said, sounding genuinely regretful as he shook his head. "There are a couple of papers being delivered at the seminar. They're important, especially if I'm going to stay on top of things. And I've got a meeting with some people who are interested in what we're doing in fiber optics."

"Aw, Nick!" Taylor left her post at the gate and came back to where Nick and Blair were standing.

In the light of a nearby street lamp, she squared her shoulders and prepared to do battle. Blair bit her tongue and watched, delighted that Taylor thought Nick's presence was that vital to their outing. Blair had already made up her own mind that Nick was a person she wanted to get to know, but it was nice to have her instincts confirmed by the one person in the world she could call family.

"You *have* to come. We were counting on it!"

"I came here to work, Taylor," Nick said firmly. "*Last* week was vacation. Now I have to earn my living." He smiled gently at the young girl, not for a moment reconsidering. Work was work and play was play—a gray area between the two simply didn't exist.

"All work and no play makes Nick a dull boy," Blair offered.

He turned on her, pulling away as he put several feet between them. "I came down here to work. That doesn't change just because you're here," he said flatly.

"I guess it doesn't." And Blair attempted to bluff her way toward hiding the pain of his rejection, although she certainly couldn't hide it from herself.

"And if I'm so dull, why didn't you go to Crete?"

"That's a low blow, Nick."

"Just a question."

"Taylor and I kind of hoped we could show you how much fun you're missing by taking yourself so seriously."

"Somebody around here has to make a living," he shot back, suddenly realizing he was on the defensive. "The company doesn't run without me."

"Have you ever tried it?" Blair asked, moving forward to touch his arm in an attempt to reach him. But he stepped back again, avoiding the contact. In the thick evening mist, she couldn't see his eyes, couldn't tell by looking at him if she'd pressed too hard—or not hard enough. So she opted for a little more pressure. "What's wrong with a healthy mix...a little fun tucked in between meetings?"

"Nothing's wrong with it. I just don't think it's my style."

"You'll never know, Nick," she said softly. "Not with that attitude."

Taylor knew when to call it quits. She mumbled good night and drifted back through the gate.

It was a standoff.

"You're stubborn as a mule." And that, she thought, was an understatement.

"Look who's talking."

"Are we going to fight about this?"

"There's nothing to fight about. I'm going to work tomorrow, and you're going to the beach." But he still wouldn't touch her, not even when she drew close enough to tempt him. Touching her, kissing her—even being near her made his willpower falter.

And it wouldn't do to let her see how sorely he was tempted.

"Guess I'll see you around, then," Blair said, shrugging her shoulders deeper into the thin sweater she'd worn, seeking warmth where there was none.

"What about dinner?"

"I thought you had to work." Her attitude resembled something close to pouting, and she knew it. But there was little she could do about it.

"Sometimes, I remember to eat—especially when I have a date with a beautiful woman."

Then again, perhaps there was hope after all. That deep, rumbling note was back in his voice, tempting her with the seductive vibrations that raced through her body. She thought about it, then nodded. Dinner wasn't everything, but it was a start. "Maybe at dinner tomorrow you'll tell me about your work."

"You really want to know?"

"Your work is what you are, Nick."

"It's not everything."

"Wanna bet?"

HE WAS WAITING for them the next morning. Not by the gate, not even at the front door.

Nick was at the breakfast table—*their* breakfast table— drinking coffee and reading the *London Times*. Dressed in casual slacks and a knit shirt, he looked ready for a day of leisure.

Her heartbeat quickened as she understood what he was doing here.

"That paper's a day old," she said, drawing his gaze as she stood at the doorway. The initial shock she'd felt at first seeing him seated there was rapidly replaced by a more pleasant sensation, one of surprise blended with a fair amount of anticipation.

"It's in English," he said easily, rising to pull out a chair beside his place at the table. He let his eyes drift over her, taking pleasure in the sight of her as she stood in the doorway. The skimpy shorts and oversize cotton shirt were almost mismatched garments that managed to tantalize even as they combined to present a respectable covering. His imagination soared as he pondered the soft curves hidden beneath the flowing shirt.

"That counts for something," she agreed, then found the strength to walk across the room to where he was standing. She stopped beside him and waited. Her eyes swept the table, noticing he'd managed to make himself right at home. The remains of his breakfast hadn't yet been cleared away, and the Plexiglas coffeepot was nearly empty.

Lifting one hand, he lightly touched her chin with his fingers, drawing her gaze to meet his. "Isn't this what you wanted?" he asked softly, tracing with his thumb the bottom lip that seemed to be on the verge of trembling.

"Yes," she whispered, then fell silent. Her eyes closed against the waves of pleasure his touch provoked, and she reveled in the pleasure he gave her so easily. Focusing on the feel of his fingers against her chin, her lips, she forgot their confrontation of the night before, banished the memory of how it had felt to say good-night without even a polite kiss between them.

She forgot it all, and concentrated on the exciting things he was making her feel now.

A soft cry escaped her lips, and Nick had to brace himself against taking more. Her mouth felt soft to his touch, and he slipped his thumb slightly inside, reveling in the wet heat he found there. He felt the tentative caress of her tongue, knew he had to stop . . . now.

It felt too good.

Regretfully, he let his hand drop away, and watched her eyes flicker open. They were clouded, almost smoky with the sensual fire she couldn't hide. Nick caught his breath and raised his hand to touch her again, to share the flames.

The noises of activity from the kitchen swept them apart. Blair sank into the chair, ignoring the sounds as Nick moved slowly back to his own seat. She was trembling, couldn't even bring herself to look at him. *How does he do it?* she asked herself for the tenth time. How did he make her feel the things she felt . . . and could he possibly feel the same?

Nick cleared his throat, determined to redirect his thoughts, and her thoughts, too, he guessed. Taylor would be joining them soon, and the day had just begun. There was a time and a place for everything. He comforted himself with that thought, then coughed again. "I thought you two were early risers."

Blair raised her eyes and easily interpreted the resolute expression in his. She nodded once, conceding the need to change speeds. "It doesn't pay to work too hard at having fun, and besides, it's only half-past eight. How'd you get past Maria Elena?" she asked, referring to the housekeeper.

"Told her we had a date."

"How did you do that? We had trouble telling her what we wanted for breakfast!" she said, awed by his achievement.

"I cheated," he said, not in the least remorseful. "The receptionist at the center wrote it down for me."

"I thought you had a meeting."

"They kicked me out when I showed up with sandals and a beach towel."

"You changed your mind?"

"I changed my mind. I rescheduled the meeting, and I can read the papers that are being presented anytime." And his tone clearly indicated she wasn't to pry further. For that matter, she wasn't to gloat over her victory, either.

Taylor bounced into the room, easily the most wide-awake person around. "What're you doing here? I thought you were chained to a desk in the monastery."

"I'm playing hooky."

"Now that's something I can relate to!" she exclaimed, flopping into the vacant chair as Maria Elena entered with their breakfast.

Nick lounged back in his chair and watched as Blair and Taylor scooped mounds of eggs and potatoes onto their plates, their appetites apparently undiminished by the previous evening's feast.

He felt a momentary panic that the picnic basket he'd brought for lunch didn't hold enough to satisfy them. But they weren't leaving civilization, he remembered. Just going to the beach.

He could always buy more.

7

"SO WHERE'S THE BEACH?" Nick looked out the window of the taxi, scanning Trapani's bustling market street for a piece of sand that was both nearby and easily reached. But so far, he hadn't seen anything that resembled the picture postcards he'd seen in the shop. Perhaps they weren't close enough yet.

The taxi had carried them down the steep, winding road from Erice to the village of Trapani, which lay at the base of the mountain. Taylor had wanted to try the cable railway that connected the two villages, but the descriptive brochure had convinced Blair she'd rather stick to the road. It was, for one thing, flatter than the almost vertical rise depicted in the color brochure.

Nick repeated his question about the beach, and Blair glanced over at him as though he were an impatient child.

"We have to work for it," she said easily, leaning forward to tap the driver on the shoulder.

He pulled to a stop next to a stand overflowing with fruits and vegetables of every description, and Nick reluctantly followed Blair and Taylor as they slid out of the taxi. Against his better judgment, he paid the man, then watched as the vehicle slipped back into traffic.

"It's that way," Blair pointed, getting his attention by grabbing a handful of his shirt and pulling him along behind a disappearing Taylor.

"So why'd we stop here?" Nick asked, wondering where "here" was.

"Because I wanted to walk through the market," Blair said innocently, deciding that now was not a good time to admit she had carefully studied the map before leaving the house. She knew where they were, even if Nick had his doubts.

Nick just shrugged, then shifted the picnic basket to his other hand so he could grab Blair's. If he was going to walk, it was going to be beside her and not trailing along behind. Besides, he admitted to himself, he wanted an excuse to hold her hand.

"What's at the end of the market?" he finally asked, handing over some change to a vendor who had convinced Taylor to buy a straw hat. It made her look a little like Tom Sawyer, but he avoided mentioning the resemblance.

"The marina," Blair said, sorting through the selection of hats to find one for herself. With the sun already hot overhead, it made sense to find a little shelter for her head.

"Thanks, Nick," Taylor said, grinning up at him from under the shaggy brim of her new hat. Then, impulsively, she crooked a finger at Nick, signaling him to bend down to her level.

On cue, Nick bent down, just in time to catch the kiss Taylor planted on his cheek. He grinned, then straightened. "You're welcome, midget," he said, glad he hadn't mentioned anything about Tom Sawyer.

As if embarrassed by the demonstration of affection, Taylor turned and loped away. Nick watched until she was swallowed up by the crowd before returning his attention to Blair.

"The marina?" he repeated, wondering if he'd heard her right.

"The marina," Blair said again, finally deciding against a hat for herself. Perhaps there'd be one she liked better farther on. "We're going to take the ferry to Levanzo."

"A ferry where?"

"To Levanzo. It's an island," Blair said patiently. "Where did you think we were going?"

"To the beach," he said suspiciously. "I thought Sicily was full of them."

"That's right," Blair agreed, responding to the twinkle in his eyes as she walked easily at his side. "But the brochure I read says the beaches on the islands nearby are less crowded. And it sounded like fun when I read about it."

She spotted the hat she wanted just a few stalls ahead, and dashed over to grab it before someone else saw it. Plopping the wide-brimmed hat over windblown curls, she dug into her pocket for some money and handed it over to the smiling girl before Nick could beat her to it.

"I like you better without a hat," he said, catching up just as the transaction finished. Sharing with her a look that made promises of a time together, he lifted a hand to tuck an errant curl behind her ear. "You've got beautiful hair, love. I like to watch it in the sun. And candlelight," he added, tipping the brim back so he could see her better. "Especially candlelight."

"What did you say?" she breathed. *Love?* Her body tingled, the excitement flowing again . . . almost as if it had never stopped. Was it always going to be this way with Nick? she wondered. What was this magic he stirred inside her?

"Something about your hair and the sun, I imagine," he murmured, dropping his fingers from her hair to trace light circles on her shoulder. "Or candlelight. I seem to have forgotten."

"You want a hat, too, mister?"

Something, it seemed, always managed to come between them. Nick sighed, then shook his head at the straw vendor and picked up the picnic basket. Snagging Blair's hand, he concentrated on their outing. "We'd better catch up with Taylor before she gets lost."

"Taylor never gets lost," Blair said, distinctly unhappy with the interruption. If it weren't for all these people, she and Nick might have a chance to finish whatever they started. She sighed and reached up to adjust the hat. A deserted beach was beginning to sound better and better.

And then, there was Taylor.

"We're almost there, Mom."

They weren't the only ones. Looking ahead, Blair could see a steady stream of foot traffic boarding the ferry. They stepped up their pace and jumped aboard just seconds before it pulled away from the dock.

"Does Mario know we're coming, Mom?" Taylor squeezed between the two adults on the salmon-colored bench and reached into the picnic basket for a handful of cookies.

"Who's Mario?" asked Nick, relieving Taylor of one of the cookies. He chewed slowly, wondering how Blair had turned a simple day at the beach into a major excursion.

"Mario is either Maria Elena's second cousin on her father's side, or is married to her sister-in-law's stepsister. I'm not sure which and I kind of gave up trying to figure it out."

"And it probably doesn't matter anyway," he suggested.

Blair grinned, pleased he was getting into the spirit of things. "Anyway, he has a fishing boat and hires it out to tourists who want to explore the island," she said. "And he speaks English," she added, crossing her fingers that Mario's English was better than the housekeeper's.

"So he'll take us to the beach?" Nick asked. After all, that was the point of the excursion.

"If we can find him. He doesn't have a phone, so Maria Elena couldn't call ahead."

Blair didn't appear to be at all disturbed by the rather loose arrangements, so Nick held his questions about Plan B for later—when they failed to locate this Mario.

The ferry slid into its berth a few minutes later, and they disembarked with the rest of the tourists. Scanning the small harbor, Blair noticed a variety of boats tied to the dock, fishing vessels mixed in with sleeker sailboats and a few rather dashing power cruisers. It was the fishing boats they were interested in, and the trio made its way across the slats that passed for a dock.

"How do we find him?" Nick asked no one in particular.

"We keep asking until we find someone that speaks English," Blair responded. "And if his name is Mario, we're set."

The man on the first boat spoke Italian, and only Italian.

The owner of the second boat spoke French, and Taylor tried to persuade Blair and Nick to forget Mario in favor of the Frenchman. But Blair held firm, promising Taylor they'd come back if Mario wasn't available. Nick sighed in relief, mostly because he was tired of not knowing what Taylor was saying. It wasn't that he didn't trust the young girl, but it made sense to remove temptation from her reach. He just didn't want to end up spending the night on the island because Taylor thought it was a neat trick. He could afford to take one day off from the conference, not two!

They hit pay dirt on the third try. Mario shook hands all around, asked in almost perfect English about his stepmother's niece, Maria Elena, and introduced them to his son, Jimmy.

"Jimmy?" Blair repeated, shaking the young man's hand as she unsuccessfully tried to curb her curiosity.

"His mama is English," Mario said, grinning at their confusion. "She named him after her father."

"Of course," Blair said. The Italian boy with an English name now made perfect sense. She understood how names were passed down from father to son. "Taylor is named after her grandfather."

"But she's a girl," Jimmy pointed out. "What's she doing with a boy's name?"

"What's wrong with my name?" challenged Taylor, moving forward in an aggressive stance that threw caution to the wind.

Blair quickly drew Nick away, taking the hand Mario offered to board the fishing boat. Nick was reluctant to follow, but she was insistent, pulling at his shirt when he paused to watch the action.

"She's been standing up for herself for years," Blair said evenly, holding Nick back when the children's voices raised and quickened. "If you interfere, she'll lose confidence."

"Don't you think she's kind of young to have to fight off a bully like that?" he accused, staying beside her even though his eyes were glued to the kids. "Just because you're so damned independent doesn't mean she has to be the same way," he said aggressively, sparing her a quick glance before returning his gaze to Taylor. "She's only a child."

"And she's *my* child, Nick." Her words were soft-spoken, but carried an unmistakable thread of steel. "Don't interfere."

It suddenly occurred to him that Jimmy's father hadn't stepped in to stop the fight, either. He could no longer hear what the children were saying, his attention was fixed on Blair. He'd known she was strong, but hadn't realized how strong.

And he'd known she loved her daughter. But until now, he hadn't known how much. Standing quietly before him, Blair held her own, determined to live life her way, and allow her daughter to do the same. Sure, Taylor might be a child, but she was growing up in a world that demanded much of its children.

Blair was giving her a place in that world. A secure place, one that was cushioned in a mother's love, but also one that would allow her to grow and learn.

"Is it hard to do that?" he asked finally, giving her hand a slight squeeze.

"Yes," she said, then tried to hide the sigh of relief that he understood. The compassion in his gaze warmed her, gave her strength to bolster her own confidence. "It's one of the hardest things about being a parent."

"I don't know if I could do it."

"It takes practice," Blair admitted, noticing the shouting match had reached a conclusion. Glancing over at Mario, they exchanged a smile of mutual relief when the kids clambered aboard the vessel. They were chatting now, Taylor saying something about Kirchberg and Jimmy offering to teach her how to steer the

boat. Mario grinned back, then winked his understanding before he bent down to start the motor. The
boat smelled of fish, naturally, but no one seemed to
mind. Blair and Nick settled down on a well-worn
bench as Taylor busied herself following the sun-
tanned boy around. When Jimmy's chores on deck were
finished, he took over the wheel, steering the boat with
much the same confidence displayed by his father.
Mario just grinned, proud of his son and wanting the
world to know it.

"Where, precisely, is he taking us?" Nick couldn't re-
sist asking. Blair had handled the finer points of their
excursion while Nick and Taylor had retreated to a fruit
stand for something to nibble on. Peeling away the last
of the rind, he pulled off a section of orange and offered it to Blair.

She took it, popping the thing whole into her mouth
because she was thirsty. . . before she realized how big
it was. And juicy.

Nick watched, fascinated, as juice dribbled out the
corner of her mouth and down her chin. She lifted a
hand to rub away the evidence of her greed, but he
stopped her, holding her wrist lightly...but firmly, just
in case she didn't understand.

He took another section of orange and pushed it between her lips, watching as she drew the soft pulpy fruit
past her teeth. Again it was too much for her mouth,
and some of the juice escaped. For a moment, he
thought about licking away the stream of juice, drawing his tongue in a long, leisurely movement across her
chin, up to her lips.

He wanted to do it, but didn't dare. Hungrily watching as her tongue darted out to take ineffectual swipes
at the sticky mess, he let her know it.

"Hey, Mom!"

It was that voice again. Nick was beginning to relate it to the Voice of Reason.

"Mom!" Taylor gave up yelling from her seat across the boat and scurried over to where Blair and Nick were attempting to clean the mess from her chin with the edge of his shirt. She watched the pair in some fascination, then said "no napkin, huh?" before crowding onto the bench between them.

Reluctantly Nick let himself be pushed aside.

"Jimmy wants me to go with them after they let you off," she said, capturing a section of orange from Nick's fingers. "There are some caves they like to dive around, and Mario says it's okay."

"Sure, it's okay," Mario said before either Nick or Blair could answer. "And I know a great beach where we can leave you on the way," he continued, "as long as you don't need to buy anything. It's pretty secluded."

"How secluded?" Nick asked, suddenly interested.

"You're stuck there until I pick you up," the other man said, grinning at Nick's expression. "The only access is by boat, and it's kind of out-of-the-way. In fact," he continued, "I've never seen anyone else stop there."

"I really don't think . . ." Blair began, less nervous about leaving Taylor than she was about being alone with Nick. Alone, with no more interruptions. She trembled, just a little, the nervous tension not an unpleasant feeling.

"Oh, Mom," Taylor argued, "I really want to go. Jimmy says the caves are really neat and we can swim all day and I'll eat with them and everything."

"Mario, it's truly kind of you to offer but I'm sure you don't want to spend your day being a . . ." And she paused, mostly because she didn't want to use the word baby-sitter and didn't know how to avoid it.

"Having someone along to play with my Jimmy would, how do you say it, 'make my day?'"

"Sounds like a winner to me," Nick said lightly, deliberately refusing to meet her gaze. He concentrated on the hazy line between sea and sky, consumed by a breathless need he could barely control. With Taylor out of the way, there was nothing to stop him from exploring the sizzling energy that flowed between them.

Would sex with Blair be as wild and erotic as he imagined? Nick nearly groaned aloud, then shifted uncomfortably. He went back to watching the sea and tried counting waves as he listened to the conversation around him.

Blair gave Nick a long look, measuring his almost casual response against her own urge to agree. It didn't make sense to say no to Taylor, she knew. She'd be safe with Mario and Jimmy, and would certainly enjoy herself more playing with someone her own age.

She gave in, gracefully. "It's a deal, Mario," Blair agreed over Taylor's giggles. "But don't tell me I didn't warn you."

Mario just laughed and checked his watch. "We'll drop you off in about fifteen minutes, then pick you up about four. And don't worry about Taylor. She'll be okay with us. The caves are really quite safe. I've known them all my life."

Nick thought about the orange he'd dropped into the lunch basket and smiled.

"WHAT NOW?" Blair asked.

"I guess we strip," he said matter-of-factly. Then he unbuttoned his slacks and let them drop to the deck.

"You *do* have a swim suit of some sort under there, don't you?" he asked, indicating the shorts and top she still wore as he pulled the knit shirt from his shoulders.

Blair just nodded, then mechanically began to undo the fastenings of her clothes. He startled her. Even when he was teasing, it was impossible to ignore the flash of excitment his husky words managed to ignite.

And now, he was teasing—more or less. The tiny cove was just as secluded as Mario had promised. Ringed on the land side by steep, jagged rocks, it was also a challenge to reach by boat. And once Mario had gained access to the cove, they still had to wade ashore. They decided to leave their clothes on the boat, and slipped into the waist-deep water, Nick shouldering the picnic basket and Blair hefting the beach towels high over her hat.

They made it to dry sand just in time to wave to the disappearing adventurers. Blair let her hand fall slowly, reluctant to acknowledge the boat was out of sight.

"I still think we should have left her some lunch," she said, staring at the gap in the rocks through which the boat had left the cove. "What if she gets hungry?" she asked quietly, almost to herself.

"Stop worrying about Taylor." Nick chucked her under the chin, bringing a smile with his easy kidding. "Mario said they had plenty on board."

"He's never fed Taylor before!" Blair retorted, shrugging away the niggling worry as she turned her back on the water and moved farther up the sandy beach.

"I suspect Jimmy gives a good imitation of a bottomless pit," Nick argued, following her a few feet before dropping the picnic basket to the sand. Together they spread the towels and organized everything to their satisfaction. With only a picnic basket and a couple of towels to arrange, it didn't take long.

Nick watched as Blair knelt beside the basket and tugged a corner of the towel until it stretched tautly over the heated sand. She was fidgeting, he realized. He didn't blame her. The combination of sun and sand and privacy was almost overwhelming—and the sensual mood they'd shared on the boat was rapidly disintegrating.

There was a decided lack of spontaneity, he mused, turning from the enticing sight of her scantily clad figure to scan the beach. He wasn't immune to the sensual draw of her creamy skin and modest curves. Out of the mood perhaps, but certainly not immune.

Blair watched him walk away.

She was shaking, just below the surface. It didn't matter that she was a mature woman with a child of her own. Logic had no part in her emotional reaction.

And it wasn't as though this was the first time she'd made love with a man.

It just felt like it.

Determined to show Nick that she knew what she was doing here with him, *wanted* to be here with him, Blair rose and moved to where he stood at the water's edge. Tentatively she rested her fingers on his shoulder, seeking reasurrance, finding his heat.

"No."

"No?" Blair repeated the word, uncertain of what it meant . . . almost afraid to find out.

"No." He turned, catching her falling hand with his own. "We're going to do this my way."

"Your way?" she asked, nervously licking her lips as she stood still under his steady gaze.

"Yes," he said evenly. "My way. Then maybe this won't feel so much like we've checked into a fleabag motel with a vibrating bed and dirty movies on the TV."

She laughed, startled by his analysis of the heavy atmosphere in the cove. Tearing her gaze away to take another look at the blue skies, blue-green water and sparkling sand, she sighed in agreement. It *was* tacky—not the beach, but the way they'd shoved Taylor aside and grabbed this opportunity with only one thought in mind.

"How did you know what I was feeling?" she asked, thankful for the telepathy or insight that had led him to that conclusion.

"Because I feel the same," he said, looking at the fingers that rested quietly in his hand before returning his gaze to her eyes. He chose his words carefully, because it was important she understood. "Sex is something that can be done anywhere, anytime. But making love is a kind of involvement, almost a seduction of the senses that plays on emotions . . . uses them to make it right."

"And you don't want to have sex with me?" she asked hesitantly, feeling her way through this new perspective he was sharing with her.

"I want to make love to you," he said bluntly. "And if you're nervous or upset or unsure . . . if I'm nervous or upset or unsure, then it won't work. It'll just be sex—and that's not enough this time."

"And how do we get it to work?" It was good, she thought, hearing Nick admit to a few inhibitions, a few insecurities. It gave her a sense of security to know he could be as vulnerable as she.

"On the boat, I was ready then," he admitted huskily, recalling the image of the drops of juice on her creamy skin, and the things he'd wanted to do to her at that moment. "And if I think about *that* fantasy too hard, I'll be ready again."

"So think about it," she suggested, finding herself recalling those few moments with a sense of heightened awareness.

"Later," he said firmly. "For now, we'll try something else."

"Another fantasy?" she asked, not convinced the first one was totally inadequate for their purposes. She was beginning to warm to him again, to feel his heat in all those places that reminded her she was a woman.

"A small one," he admitted, the corner of his mouth edging upward. "I think you'll like it."

"I've never shared a fantasy with a man before," she said softly, drawing her tongue along lips that were suddenly dry.

"Good," he said, the satisfaction clear in his voice. "This will be a new experience for you."

"What is it?" she demanded, suddenly anxious to begin.

"We'll pretend Taylor is here."

This was not what she expected. Blair choked back a laugh, then let it out when she saw the determined look on his face. Pretend Taylor was with them? "And what, precisely, will *that* accomplish?" she asked, her own smile widening in response to his.

"With Taylor as chaperon we can go back to having fun and sneaking an occasional leer."

"And what if I want more?" she asked, her voice a silken temptation he found hard to ignore.

"Please, Blair," he warned, looking over his shoulder as if to make sure Taylor wasn't close enough to listen. "Remember the child. Tender ears and all that," he cautioned, dropping her hand as she moved a step closer to him. Wagging his finger in her face, he took two giant steps backward.

"You're serious about this!" she suddenly realized.

"Of course, I'm serious!" he said, then raised his voice just enough to include his chaperon in the conversation. "Come on, Taylor. I'll race you across the water!" But he didn't dash into the waves, not yet. He wanted to see what Blair would do about their newly arrived guest.

"Is it sunstroke?" she quizzed, matching Nick step for step as he backed slowly into the warm waters.

"What sunstroke?" he denied, careful to stay out of her reach. "You think I can't beat her?"

"We should have bought you a hat," Blair said, not taking her eyes off his retreating form. "A pity the local umbrella merchant seems to have missed this stretch of beach."

"Taylor says I can borrow hers," he countered, then waited for Blair to argue against that logic. He was waist deep in the water by then, and she was closing in. He thought he caught a glimpse of malicious mischief in her eyes, but he could have been mistaken.

He doubted it.

Gentle waves lapped at her breasts, almost distracting her with their persistence as she tracked Nick. But she was determined, and that made all the difference in the world. "I think your imagination needs a good soaking," she said, calculating the distance between them. She made a broad, sweeping motion over the surface of the water, barely creating a ripple between them. She did it again, this time launching a small wave that broke at his shoulders.

"I'll have you know Taylor is fighting on my side," he warned as she raised her arm to make another wave.

She paused for a moment, then shrugged, apparently unconcerned at being outnumbered. "It's your fantasy. If you want to hide behind an eleven-year-old girl, that's your privilege."

He edged backward, moving more rapidly when he discovered the seabed didn't drop off as dramatically as he would have hoped. He was still chest deep in the water, meaning Blair could easily stand up and fight.

The odds would be better if he was standing while she had to tread water. Not fair, he admitted, but certainly more interesting.

"Chester Nicholas Dalton, come back here and fight like a man!"

"Careful, Blair," he cautioned, abruptly backing away as she lunged in his direction. "You wouldn't want to get Taylor's hat all wet, would you?"

"I don't give a—" she began before she was cut off.

"Blair! Mind your tongue!"

She thought fast, then made the appropriate substitution. "As I was saying before I was so rudely interrupted, I don't give a goose about Taylor's hat! It's your sanity that I'm worried about."

"Give a goose?" He laughed then, the rich notes echoing heavily throughout the cove.

"An old family saying," she ad-libbed, then pushed a small wall of water in his direction.

He ducked the onslaught, realizing his tactical error when water filled his ears and nostrils.

Blair giggled as he slowly surfaced, blowing water out his mouth and wiping the stinging saltwater from his eyes. She thought she could detect smoke coming out of his ears, but didn't want to get close enough to make sure. As it was, his eyes took on a vaguely menacing look, and she abruptly forgot the laughter and worried about survival. Electing to run and live to swim another day—or swim and live to run another day—she pushed away from the sandy seabed and struck out for safer waters, kicking frantically as her arms dug into the buoyant water.

It was the additional insult of having water kicked in his face that aroused his killer instincts. Nick snagged her by the ankle before she could make good her escape, then reeled her in, easily overcoming her efforts to escape.

Moving hand over hand, he worked his way steadily up her body. Gaining a firm hold on first one knee and then the other, he tucked her flailing legs under his arm and grasped her hip. It was slippery there, and his fingers dug into the seam of her bikini bottoms for something to hang on to.

It was blind luck that they didn't come off.

Blair gasped when he began to tug, swallowing a mouthful of water as he drew her steadily back to his chest. She couldn't struggle, not then. She was too busy trying to keep her head above water as he dragged her backward. Even that was taking a chance with fate because with his fingers wrapped around that strip of fabric clinging precariously to her hip, it was dangerous to do much more than breathe—and pray he wouldn't decide to go ahead and drown her.

But then he wouldn't dare any such thing . . . not in front of Taylor.

He stopped when her waist was firmly secured between his arm and side, releasing his hold on her bikini in the same second that he flipped her onto her back. He held her there, firmly resisting her efforts to stand. With one hand at her shoulder and the other riding lightly on her waist, he gentled her.

"I could make you pay for that, you know," he murmured, lowering his head until their lips were just
inches apart. He stopped there, dragging his gaze over
her mouth again and again, as if wondering where to
begin his assault.

Blair gasped, and sensed this was the moment she'd
been waiting for. Closing her eyes as if she was over-
come with emotion, she took several careful breaths,
releasing them slowly so as not to warn him. Her arms
began gentle treading movements in the water, each
stroke slightly wider than the last.

And then she was ready.

"Jump him, Taylor!" she shouted, thus confusing the
issue for the precious moments she needed. After all,
Taylor was supposed to be on *his* side! Then pushing
with all her strength against the barrier of water, she
created a storm that caught Nick at its center and
drenched him completely. The surprise also purchased
her release, and Blair wasted no time in leaving the
scene of the crime. Stroking frantically toward the far
end of the cove where jagged rocks guarded the entrance, she swam as if there were sharks nipping at her
feet.

Sharks, perhaps, might have been more merciful.

She could hear him behind her, closing in. She didn't
have a chance, not even half a chance. But she didn't
give up. Stroke after stroke, she pulled her body
through the water. The rocks were getting closer now.
She could almost feel their rough texture under her feet.

And she nearly made it.

This time Nick didn't bother with grabbing an ankle. He swam until he was beside her, then passed her,
easily reaching the rocks before her. Hauling himself up
on a narrow ledge, he waited, his attitude a deliberate

parody of Taylor and Blair's routine when they would beat him to the bottom of a ski slope.

"What took you so long?" he asked, coming down to rest on his haunches as Blair began to tread water.

When he didn't immediately stretch out a hand to help her up, she knew he was going to let her drown. Or swim all the way back to the beach. Blair thought about it, and decided to play on his guilt.

"I had to wait for Taylor," she said easily. "She hasn't been swimming in a while . . . I thought one of us had better stay with her." There was a distinct note of reprimand in her voice by the time she finished, and Nick had the grace to look somewhat chagrined.

"I suppose you want to come up on my rock," he said, holding out a hand to her.

"Your rock?"

"I don't see *your* footprints all over it," he pointed out.

Blair decided not to argue about it. She was getting tired, and sitting down became a priority. She took the hand he offered, allowing Nick to pull her out of the water and onto his rock. He released her the moment she steadied herself, and dived cleanly into the water before she had a chance to sit down.

"You two have a rest," he suggested when he surfaced. "I'm going back for the orange."

"Orange?" But he was already gone, stroking smoothly and rapidly toward their encampment on the shore. Blair just shook her head, delighted with the spray of water that flew out of her hair. She shook it again, wondering if she resembled a dog shedding water after a swim, or just felt like one! She chuckled, shaking her head a final time before lifting her face to the bright warmth of the sun.

An orange? She laughed. First the fantasy with Taylor as chaperon, now something about an orange. Nick certainly wasn't doing anything predictable, she thought. But he was making her comfortable—with him, with the situation.

He was giving her a choice.

Blair knew she'd already made that choice, but she was grateful all the same. Knowing what she wanted...and being able to reach out and take it...well, they were two different things.

Earlier, on the beach, when she'd tried to force a beginning, Blair had been just about as uncomfortable as could be imagined. Wanting to be with him, alone with him, had nothing to do with what was happening now. Not only had Nick sensed that, he had appeared to have a few uncomfortable moments himself.

But he was working to make it better. Thus the fantasy.

Opening her eyes to see him swimming back to her, she wondered again what the orange had to do with anything.

BLAIR MOANED, then swallowed the chocolate-covered sweet before it melted on her lips. She moaned again, holding her hands over her stomach in protest.

"Come on, Blair," Nick goaded, "you can do better than that!"

"No, I can't! Honest!" she vowed, rolling her head sideways on the towel as Nick tried to push another sweet into her mouth. "Give it to Taylor. She loves chocolate-covered truffles."

Nick just shook his head in mock disgust. "Taylor already had her share. I just want to be sure you don't go hungry."

"Hungry!"

"Well, you said you were starved after the diving contest," he pointed out. "And then we spent another fifteen minutes bobbing for the orange before lunch. I just want to be sure you're full."

"I'm full," she groaned, then rolled to a sitting position before he could stuff anything else into her mouth. "But I'm thirsty as all get-out. What do you have in there besides coffee?"

"Champagne for us, soda for the midget."

"Champagne?" she echoed, glancing over at the picnic basket. Blair wrinkled her nose at the thought of warm champagne, then stood and brushed the sand from her thighs. She was hot, and a quick rinse in the water seemed a good idea. "That's a wonderfully decadent thing to bring on a picnic, but warm champagne sounds incredibly disgusting right now."

"Who said anything about 'warm' champagne?" Nick asked, then reached inside the basket to extract a bottle completely wrapped in a heavy sack. "This is one of my company's products." He kneaded the rubbery material, and Blair heard the crunch of tiny glass vials inside the fabric of the bag.

"There. A few chemical reactions, a bit of thermodynamics, and—ta da—cold champagne!"

Blair was intrigued. Dropping down to kneel in the sand beside him, she waited impatiently for him to pull the bottle out of the sack. But when she reached her hand out to feel the cool bottle, he stopped her.

"Don't!" And he held the bottle just out of her reach. "Don't touch. Not yet."

Blair raised her eyebrows inquiringly, torn between obeying his command and ignoring it altogether. She was hot and thirsty. Moisture was beginning to bead on the outside of the bottle as the sun began to warm it. She felt a bead of perspiration form on her lip, and her tongue darted out to soak up the salty drop.

She wanted to touch the bottle, to cool herself with the sparkling liquid inside.

Instead, she did as Nick asked. She waited.

And watched.

Slowly, deliberately, Nick brought the unopened bottle back within her reach. He paused then, keeping his steady gaze on her face. "Close your eyes."

"Why?"

"Because I want you to."

"What about Taylor?" Blair teased, debating whether to grab the bottle and run, or do as he asked. "Does she have to close her eyes, too?"

"Taylor isn't here anymore."

Blair gasped, her heart nearly tripping over itself in a sudden rush that pushed the blood into her face. He hadn't taken his eyes off her, and she felt their heavy weight blazing deep into her soul.

"Now. Close your eyes, Blair," he commanded softly, the gravelly voice at once stern and incredibly provocative.

Almost against her will, Blair allowed her eyelids to drift shut.

Nick didn't wait for more than an instant. Drawing himself up on his knees, he closed the distance between them. He knew she felt the movement, felt her flinch just slightly when his thighs closed in around hers.

And then, before she could open her eyes, he pressed the bottle of champagne hard against the naked skin of her belly.

8

IT WAS ANOTHER fantasy now.

Her eyes flew open; the cold bottle against her bare stomach created an incredibly shocking erotic sensation. She gasped, then threw back her head and arched against it, fighting against the urge to shrink away.

She forgot her thirst.

She reveled in the heat that was filling her breasts, making them heavy with need. Digging her hands deep into the sand at her side, she arched again, and this time knew the liquid fire between her legs would not simply go away by ignoring it.

This time, she was ready. Lifting her head, she met his gaze.

He was burning for her, but still he waited. He measured her response by her eyes, satisfied to see they were clouded with passion and need. By shifting the bottle just a few inches, it came to rest between her breasts. He heard the sharp intake of breath, and wondered if the cold moisture had caused it, or if she was more aware of his fingers that grazed the silky curve of her breast.

He rubbed the bottle up and down slowly, drawing his forefinger along the edge of her bikini top with each stroke. Taking his eyes from her he watched her reaction. The evidence of her need was obvious; her nipples were beginning to push against the thin fabric. She held her breath each time he neared a pointed tip, only letting it out when he passed it without touching.

He watched her for a moment, enjoying the arousal she couldn't hide from him. And he remembered how they had played together in the water, recalled the moment when he'd felt her tremble at his touch, the way her body had gone rigid as he smoothed past her thighs to reach her hips before he'd snagged her by her bikini bottoms.

He'd wanted her then. But not as much as he wanted her now. He was glad they'd waited.

"You're so hot the champagne is getting warm," he murmured, then dipped his head and put his mouth on her, drawing a hardened bud between his teeth.

Blair couldn't stop the low moan that originated somewhere deep inside. Instead she let it come, and then again. With his teeth gently pulling at her breast, her whole being was suddenly reduced to pleasure—his and hers.

Still grasping handfuls of sand, she raised her arms and opened her fingers against his shoulders. The sand sifted onto his shoulders, his back, and away. Her fingers brushed at it with soft motions, delighting in the way his muscles bunched and rippled beneath her movements. She concentrated hard, continuing the tiny brushing motion down over his chest.

His mouth left her breast and she cried out, the protest changing to a moan of pleasure as he simply moved to her other nipple. She arched back again, almost losing her balance against the incredible excitement of his mouth. But he caught her, dropping the bottle to the sand and hooking an arm behind her back. His hand came to rest at her hip, familiarly snagging a hold in the slip of material that rested there.

He didn't stop there, just paused long enough to remind her of that other time.

He touched her lightly, trailing his fingers across her tummy as he teased the barrier of cloth that covered her most secret place. She felt the first flutter of her stomach clenching as first one finger, then another dipped past the seam, before retreating to caress the sensitive skin between her thighs.

With the fingers of his other hand, he rimmed the edge of the bikini top, toying with it, driving her mad with the need to feel him—his mouth, his hands—against her bare breast. She wanted to tell him, but the words were stuck behind the need to breathe. So she dragged her fingers through his hair, holding him close for just a moment before she pulled him away.

"I can't stand any more." She was breathing raggedly, knew she wouldn't have been able to continue kneeling before him without his support. And that look in his eyes was making her melt, so full of fire and need and desire.

"Yes, you can," he murmured, then slipped the straps from her shoulders and let them drift down to her elbows. "You can take a lot. You have to."

"But I want—"

And he hushed her with his fingers, holding them there for just a moment before letting them drift to rest on the fastener between her breasts. "I know you want it. So do I," he whispered, dragging his eyes from hers as he watched his fingers deal with the tiny buckle. "But I want this, too," he said. "I want to see every part of you, touch you . . . taste you."

Dragging his gaze upward one last time, he finished. "I want it all . . . and I want it slowly." He took a deep breath, saw the smoldering fire she couldn't control and

smiled, just a little. "I'm not saying this is the easy way
to do it, but I think you'll like it, love. Say you'll be pa-
tient, hmmm?"

Blair swallowed, briefly wondered where he got such
incredible control when all she wanted was to feel him
sheathed deep inside her, plunging with her over the
edge of oblivion. She didn't want to go alone, but his
hands, his mouth . . . they could send her there easily.

"I don't know how long I can wait."

The truth was almost his undoing. He could take her
now, strip away the last barriers between them and
push himself inside her . . . and, in seconds, it would be
over.

"You don't have to wait. For me, perhaps, yes," he
said softly, cupping her chin as he grazed her lips with
his. "But no one said you could only see the stars just
once today. I'll show you a galaxy."

And he thrust his tongue past her teeth, driving so
deeply that she felt she was drowning in his taste. But
she held on, moving her head to give him better access,
digging her fingers into the corded muscles of his
shoulder.

It was incredible, these promises he made. The excitement poured through her, and still she was startled
to feel his fingers move over the fastening between her
breasts. Why the surprise? she wondered, breathing
deeply when he pulled his head back.

The material fell away from her breasts, and the jut-
ting nipples were finally bared for his greedy eyes. He
watched as his fingers traced a curving line toward the
dark rose points, felt his heart slam against his ribs
when his thumb finally reached the eager nubs and
flicked them gently.

Blair watched spellbound as he leaned toward her once again, this time bringing his open mouth to rest on the straining buds. Her arms clenched, then fell loosely across his shoulders as he drew her breast into his mouth, the erotic suction wiping away all thoughts and replacing them with feeling and . . . passion.

She stayed with him, followed his lead, breathed when she had to, cried out when she couldn't help it. His hands were everywhere, followed by his lips, his mouth.

He explored her, discovered her secrets, laid bare her feminine mysteries and left his mark on them. It was an intimate revelation of such sensual delight that she couldn't imagine ever sharing this with any other man. He was her natural partner, chosen out of millions to share in her pleasure and take his own in return.

He was a man she could love.

It took her breath away. Blair tried to speak, to tell him, but he was oblivious to her thoughts. He was totally involved in the physical pleasure they were sharing.

Talking could wait, she decided, mostly because she was helpless to do otherwise.

She trembled at his determination to know everything, to see it all, to touch it, taste it. She lay back on the towel to make it easier for him . . . to keep from falling. Nick slipped off what was left of their clothes, and she gasped to see the proud masculinity of him, reached out to touch, was disappointed when he evaded her fingers.

Nick shuddered at the close call, then gathered her body close, tangling their limbs as he learned the feel of her. She wanted to touch, but he'd had to stop her, prolonging his own pleasure—and hers—by reserving the ultimate caress a few moments longer. A single stroke from her would send him reeling, and he wasn't ready. Not yet.

Not even when she cried out as he pushed her to the stars. Again and again, he drove her upward never giving her a chance to recover before starting again, sending her spinning out of control, maintaining such a high pitch of excitment that the sweat flowed freely off her skin.

She thrashed, and he held her steady for his touch.

She bucked, but his fingers didn't pause in their silky caress.

She strained against his hands, pushed against his mouth, and finally, won the battle. With fingers that were at once gentle and demanding, she found the hard center of him that was straining against the cruelty of delay.

He quit thinking then. Sliding into the cradle of her thighs and pushing himself into her hot, welcoming body, he gave himself to the exquisite pleasure of learning her last secret. Resting for a moment, he let himself be absorbed by her warmth. He gathered his energy, prepared himself to drive her slowly to the final rapture.

But she didn't want him to rest. He felt the feminine muscles contract around him, and knew her patience was at an end.

Blair gathered the last of her strength and lifted her hips against him, daring him to take it slowly. She drew back quickly, then lifted up again, inviting him deeper into her warmth. She was exhausted, and exhilarated. But he'd taught her something, and she was determined to use it.

He'd taught her to make her own demands, that greed was exciting. She wanted him hard and fast and hot, not slow and gentle.

And she took him that way. Hard. And fast. And hot....

"WHATEVER GAVE ME the idea I was in control back there?" he asked, rolling off her before his weight crushed the very life from her body. Even in the bright sun, he suddenly felt miserably cold. So he pulled her to lay on top of him, pleased when she snuggled her face into his chest and draped her legs around his thighs.

"Control is a figment of the imagination," she said smoothly, then took another deep breath to support her next sentence. "And losing it is kind of exciting, too."

She could feel the laughter inside him, would have responded with her own had she not been so completely exhausted. Even the caress of his fingers at the base of her spine failed to ignite the fires within, and she merely accepted the light touch as a reminder of his presence—as if she could forget!

"We're going to get burned," he said, too weary to do much about it. "Especially those places we didn't put any lotion on."

"I don't see what you're worried about," Blair joked, stretching her legs to ease the pleasantly aching muscles before resettling them around his. "I'm the one that's going to get burned. There's nothing of you for the sun to get a peek at."

"If you grab the lotion, I'll give you a hand," he offered, suddenly intrigued by the possibilities.

Blair felt a sudden thrill race through her, then almost fainted at what it meant. She was too exhausted to want him again, she reasoned. She needed a rest, a nap if she could manage it. But her nipples defiantly tightened, and she rubbed them against his chest, enjoying the stimulation of her tender flesh against the slightly abrasive hairs that curled there.

The faint stirring in his loins astonished Nick, making him realize he needed her again . . . that once was only a beginning. But it was the fact that he wanted her now, immediately, that surprised him.

Reaching up to cup her chin, he took her lips gently. "Let's do the lotion first," he suggested.

"THEY WERE SUPPOSED to be here by four."

Blair just nodded from under her hat. She wasn't worried. Instinct had told her to trust Mario, and she saw no reason to re-evaluate. She'd learned to trust her instincts, and wouldn't have let Taylor go with Mario and Jimmy if there had been the slightest doubt in her mind. No, they might be late, but they'd be here. Eventually.

In the meantime, she wished Nick would settle down beside her so they could talk . . . about that wonderful thing she'd discovered she felt about him. Love, she thought, smiling at the goose bumps the word incited. The how and why of it all pretty much mystified her, but the reality was there. And she wanted to share it with Nick.

He'd used the word "love" several times already, she reminded herself. Surely he wasn't a man to throw around serious words like that without meaning them.

If he'd just sit down, they could talk.

Checking his watch for the twelfth time in as many minutes, he resumed pacing up and down in front of the towels where Blair sprawled. "He said four o'clock. It's nearly five."

Blair sighed and pushed herself up to lean on her elbows, smothering the temptation to stroke her fingers up the strong muscles of his legs. He had stopped her the last time she tried that, pointing out that Taylor and the rest might arrive any moment.

"Why don't you just relax and have the rest of the champagne," she suggested. "They'll be along soon."

"But they're already an hour late," he persisted, glancing back at the rocks on the off chance they'd entered the cove since he'd turned away.

Blair decided a little reassurance was in order. "There's nothing to worry about, Nick. They're probably just having a good time and aren't watching the clock," she soothed, pushing her hat back on her head so she could look at him. "Besides, time doesn't mean as much here as it does in New Jersey," she added, totally incapable of omitting the sarcastic jibe.

She might be in love with him, but those nasty little habits such as clock watching were part of a life-style that had to go! Blair was already planning her strategy for eradicating the workaholic tendencies from Nick's life.

"I'd think you'd be a little more worried about your daughter and less concerned with scoring points off me," he shot back.

"And I'd say you've got the worry square nicely covered," she replied. Blair was pretty sure she resented Nick's accusation, and she certainly didn't like the way this conversation was turning into an argument. "And Taylor is *my* daughter. If there's any worrying to be done, I'll do it."

"For a mother, you're remarkably casual about the welfare of your child." He stopped pacing then, confronting her with his hands on his hips and an accusing gleam in his eyes. "Or is not worrying just part of your life-style now that you've given up a permanent home and a job."

That did it! This wasn't an argument. It was a full-fledged battle. Blair slowly drew herself up to face him, straining her calves as she rose onto the balls of her feet to gain a couple more inches.

"So we're back to that, are we?" she bit out, clenching her hands at her sides and barely restraining the impulse to physically hit back.

"Face it, Blair," he said. "If your life-style was more conventional, you wouldn't have problems like this to worry about."

"You're out of line, Nick," she warned. "And you're not even making sense. What has where we live got to do with anything? We're here on vacation. Lots of people go on vacation. Kids meet other kids all the time and go off and play together."

"True," he conceded. "But it's not every parent that has to worry about whether sending their daughter off with a Sicilian fisherman is a good idea or not."

"I'm not worried," she reminded him evenly. "You are. And if you thought Mario couldn't be trusted, then why did you encourage me to let Taylor go in the first place?"

He opened his mouth to answer, but nothing came out. Angrily he swung away, returning to the shoreline where he resumed his pacing.

That was it, she realized. He wasn't mad at her, he was mad at himself. Blair sat back on the towel and wondered how long it would take for him to realize it.

She also wondered if she could forget the accusations he'd made, or if she really wanted to.

"I DIDN'T MEAN IT. Not any of it."

She hadn't seen him approach, couldn't help the tremor that shook her as he knelt down beside her. She took cover behind sarcasm, disguising the hurt with anger and hostility. "You're not worried so much about Taylor's welfare as you are about your ride home," she said harshly.

It wouldn't take much to make her cry, she thought irrelevantly. But she was stronger than that. She had to be.

"I deserved that," he said quietly. Taking her chin in a grip that surprised her with its gentleness, he forced her eyes to meet his. "And you probably don't want to listen to me right now. I don't blame you. But this might be the only chance I get to apologize, and I'm not fool enough to let it slip through my fingers."

"Go away," she said quietly. There was a very slender thread holding her emotions together, and this sudden tenderness he was showing was enough to break it. She wanted him to go away, give her time to erect her defenses.

"There's nowhere to go," he pointed out. "And besides, I'm not letting you off this island until you hear me out."

Blair tried to jerk her chin out of his grasp, but he tightened his fingers. "Bully!"

"I can be," he admitted. "Are you ready to listen?"

"There aren't a lot of choices," she shot back, thinking about throwing sand in his face. But she didn't, mostly because he seemed to sense what she was about to do and moved his grip to her wrists.

"No, there aren't, are there?" he agreed. Holding her gaze with his own, he repeated his earlier words. "I didn't mean what I said. Not any of it. It's the guilt that's eating me up. I can't stand knowing it's my fault that Taylor is out there with a man we barely know, possibly hurt or in danger . . . God knows what else. And it's all my fault."

"I told you before. Taylor is my daughter, my responsibility," she said evenly.

"That's not the point. I pushed you into letting her go with Mario. She could have jumped overboard for all I cared. All I wanted was to be alone with you, to make love to you, and nothing else mattered."

He couldn't look at her anymore. Dropping his gaze, he took a deep breath and finished what he'd meant to say. "I suppose I was trying to shift the blame, make you feel as bad as I do."

"You succeeded." For different reasons, she thought, avoiding his eyes as he raised his head.

"I guessed that much." Letting go of her wrists, he moved to sit beside her, not touching.

She understood how he felt. It didn't change things, at least nothing that really mattered. But she understood, could even empathize with the guilt. Hadn't she felt the same way once upon a time. Blair remembered the incident that had triggered the major upheaval in her own life, in Taylor's life.

She'd been working, pretty much nonstop for several weeks. She hadn't seen Taylor, not awake, in almost a month. She'd come home early from the office, her latest project finished, the next one waiting on her desk.

She'd walked in on a birthday party. Taylor's birthday, her ninth. It wasn't so much that Blair had forgotten that hurt, it was realizing that Taylor hadn't even expected her to show up that tore her apart.

Taylor had been surprised, almost ill at ease with Blair's sudden appearance. But when the other kids had asked what she'd gotten Taylor, it had been her own daughter that made up the lie about the doll that hadn't been delivered.

Taylor had loved her even then, enough to lie to her friends.

Everything that had come since then had been an outgrowth of that one incident. The guilt that had shaken apart her world had lasted a long time, but she'd gradually gotten over it. Now her life was centered around Taylor, and she'd never forgotten her lesson.

Nick was going through something similar, and Blair couldn't help but understand. Guilt was a powerful emotion, and she could tell it was tearing him apart.

She loved him enough to help him through it. "There's nothing wrong with Taylor," she said simply.

"How can you be so sure?" he pressed, shaking his head at the fear that couldn't be dismissed.

"I can't say for sure," she started. "But the only time she's really been hurt, I knew it. She fell out of a tree, and I knew something had happened before the school called me. She had a broken arm." She shrugged, knowing he wouldn't understand. "And I trust Mario. I think you do, too. But you're feeling too guilty now to admit it."

The silence stretched between them, and she let him think about it. There wasn't much more she could add, probably nothing that would make him feel better. But she had tried, and felt better for it.

Loving Nick was such an easy thing to get used to. Not telling him was going to be the hard part.

"I wish I had your confidence right now," he finally said.

"It takes practice," she admitted, surprised to find a tiny smile tugging at the corner of her mouth.

Nick would make a wonderful father, she realized. She could picture him with children of his own, caring for them, worrying about them. She wondered if he would remember this day and his first exposure to worrying about a child. But she shook her head against the idea, realizing she might never know.

He pushed himself up to stand on his feet, brushing the sand from his legs. He offered her a hand up, trying to hide the surprise when she took it. Pulling her up beside him, he suggested, "Let's swim out to the rocks and try to catch a ride. If . . . When Mario shows up, he'll figure it out and go back without us."

"All right." And she turned away from him because she couldn't think of anything else to say.

He didn't let her get away that easily. "We've got some more talking to do, but we can take care of that later. After we find Taylor."

"I don't think there's anything left to say," she said, keeping her back to him.

"Later," he promised, ignoring her negative response.

Without a word, they gathered the bits and pieces of their picnic and tucked everything, including the towels, into the basket. Blair followed Nick into the water, swam alongside him as he alternately held the basket out of the water first with one hand, then the other. It looked like hard work, and Blair wondered why he bothered. There was certainly nothing inside that couldn't either be replaced or simply washed. But they reached their goal within minutes, and were soon perched on the rocks with mostly dry towels for cushions.

Blair stared out at the sparkling sea, wondering how long they'd have to wait, wishing she had never given into the impulse to come to Sicily.

But she'd come here willingly. She'd made love with Nick, also willingly. And she'd fallen in love with him.

In return, she thought he might care for her. But love? She didn't think so. He disapproved of her—her life-style—too much to allow himself to love her. She would have to live with that now. There weren't any other choices.

They hadn't been there two minutes before Nick jumped up and started waving his beach towel. Blair stared hard in the direction he was waving and spotted the boat he was signaling.

Rescue was at hand.

THE SUN-DRENCHED CROWD of laughing sightseers welcomed them on board without hesitation. The captain tried to discover how and why they came to be stranded, but the language problem made any normal conversation impossible and he finally gave up.

They had just rounded the tip of the island when they saw Mario's boat.

The craft was dead in the water, and Taylor was nonchalantly sitting on the foredeck with her thumb stuck out as if to hitch a ride. Nick embarked on another round of sign language that was intended to tell the captain that they wanted to approach the other boat, but the Italian was already steering toward it.

Nick wanted to share his relief with Blair. He didn't, though. Blair was still pretending he didn't exist. It had been that way since they'd boarded the crowded tourist boat. She had surrounded herself with the happy, slightly drunk tourists and engaged them in a game of charades. Nick watched her efforts to communicate the simplest words, amazed at her ability to adapt to the situation.

They were within hailing distance before Taylor recognized Nick and Blair, and she let out a whoop that brought Mario and Jimmy clambering up from the depths of the boat.

"It's the marines!" she shouted, dancing rather precariously on the deck. Jimmy joined her in the impromptu dance, and they had collapsed into giggles by the time the two boats came together.

Mario and the captain of the "rescue" boat entered into a long, involved dialogue and Nick waited impatiently for the outcome. He knew the exact moment Blair had come to stand beside him, but didn't acknowledge her presence. This was no place to talk, and there were things he had to say that were for her ears alone.

Taylor was safe, and for now, nothing else mattered.

It took at least five minutes for the two captains to make the decision to tow the disabled boat back to the dock; fixing it was apparently out of the question. Taking advantage of the side-by-side positions of the boats, Nick jumped across the narrow slice of water then held his hand out for Blair.

He could see her reluctance to accept his help, but he ignored it. When she finally made the jump, he was there to steady her.

She managed to free herself from his helping hands in two seconds flat. Then Taylor was all over them, hugging her mother, squealing delightedly when Nick swept her off her feet in a rather splendid bear hug. She babbled nonstop about their terrific day at the caves, blissfully ignorant of the strained silence between the adults. By the time she finally wound down, a line had been fixed to the bow and the tourist boat was pulling them toward Trapani.

"Can we do it again, Mom?" she begged. "Jimmy has to go back to school tomorrow, but if we stay until Saturday, he promised we could go back to the caves!" Her eyes shone with excitement, and Blair didn't have the heart to tell her no.

"We'll talk later, darling," Blair said, then drew her finger along the top of Taylor's sunburned cheeks. "Right now, all I want to think about is a bath and a cold drink."

"Okay. I'm going up front with Jimmy. He's showing me how to tie sailor's knots," she said breathlessly, then scrambled over the deck to the corner where the young boy was toying with bits of rope.

"I'm sorry I ruined it."

Blair tilted her head to look at him, surprised he'd broken the silence between them. "Excuse me?"

"It's never been like that before," he said. "Making love, I mean," he explained, seeing the confusion on her face. "It was the stuff dreams are made of," he added, almost to himself. "But I went and ruined it all. And now I don't know how to get it back."

Blair licked her lips and tried to think of something that would make him stop talking. She didn't want to hear this. "It doesn't matter," she finally said.

Nick didn't give up. Cupping her face with his open palms, he forced her to look at him, to listen. "I'm sorry."

"So am I," she breathed. So very, very sorry. And when she turned her face away, he let her go.

"This isn't over," he said softly. "Not by a long shot."

She heard the words, and knew he meant them, but she didn't turn back. She couldn't.

THEIR PLANE LEFT Crete's Iraklion airport on time, but a combination of bad weather and air traffic delayed their arrival in Brussels. By the time they'd reclaimed the car and driven the sixty-odd miles to Bruges, Blair was exhausted.

"I'll get the skis, Mom," Taylor offered as Blair popped open the trunk.

"You can get the bags, too," Blair said. "Just set them by the door while I get rid of the car. I'll bring them upstairs."

Taylor grumbled a little, but that was to be expected. The bags were heavy. Blair would have offered to help, but the narrow alley made it impossible for her to open her car door. So she sat there, wincing as Taylor scraped her boot bag over the shiny paint of the car. One of the problems of living in the old part of Bruges was that the streets hadn't been built with cars in mind, and the city's residents were constantly at odds with the cobblestone byways that paralleled the picturesque canals.

Taylor bounced the trunk shut, and Blair put the car back into gear. Three blocks away, she pulled into the tiny space she rented and locked the car. By the time she arrived back at their apartment, Taylor had managed to haul all but two cases up the steps. Blair took one in each hand and climbed the twenty-three stairs that led to her home.

"There's nothing in the fridge."

"And you're surprised?" Blair asked, grunting under the weight of the heavy cases.

"Can we go out for dinner?" Taylor asked, pursuing the subject of food as though it were the most important thing in her life.

Blair sighed and dumped the cases beside her bedroom door. Life with Taylor never changed, she thought ruefully. She always managed to reduce things to a single topic: food! "I guess we'll have to," she agreed, although it was the last thing she wanted to do. "The shops are closed now, so we'll go to the Market in the morning."

"You mean *you'll* go to the Market," Taylor corrected, throwing her lean body onto the plump cushions of the sofa. "*I* have school."

"That's right." Tomorrow was Monday, she realized. Where had time gone? "School."

She shrugged out of her coat and set to work. Moving quickly through the room, she turned on a few lights, adjusted the blinds and generally got reacquainted with the place. Then she tackled the coal furnace in the kitchen, an antiquated contraption that provided them with hot water and, not incidentally, heat for the entire apartment.

Filling the bin with coal was a daily job—twice daily in winter when the thermostat was set higher. Blair topped off the bin and then went to work getting the stuff to ignite. Once started, it would burn ad infinitum, or until she forgot to add coal. She was lucky on the second try, and soon the coals were glowing warmly.

The coal furnace aside, Blair liked their home, even if it was a little small. It had a cozy feeling to it, warm without being oppressive. The bay windows probably had something to do with that, she knew, pulling the drapes aside to look at the canal below. They'd been lucky to find a place so near the center yet on a quiet street—canal, she corrected herself. She couldn't wait until the weather warmed up enough for the flowers to come out. It would be beautiful then, she knew.

Nick would have loved it.

She caught the thought before it could go any further, and forced herself to get busy. If she stayed busy enough, there wouldn't be time to think.

"Hey, Mom?"

Blair dug into the small case she was unloading onto the kitchen table and replied without looking up. "Yes, Taylor?"

"When are you going to tell me what happened in Erice?"

Blair gasped. She'd been expecting it, but still it had taken her by surprise. She took a deep breath, trying to quell the nervousness that gripped her. Turning, she looked across the room at her daughter.

Taylor hadn't wanted to leave Erice, couldn't understand Blair's sudden urge to see Crete. But she'd gone along just the same, had even made it easier for her mother when it could have been so hard. Crete had been hot, blindingly white and incredibly beautiful. They'd spent their days together, swimming and sunning. The hotel had been small and quiet, with no one intruding on their privacy.

It had been a relaxing week.

And now Taylor had brought up the subject Blair had spent all week avoiding. She could tell her it was none of her business, but that wasn't true. Taylor was a part of this and deserved to know.

After all, if things had worked the way Blair had dreamed, Nick might have been her stepfather. For just those few hours on that deserted beach, Blair had dared to imagine the three of them together as a family.

But dreams got smashed sometimes. Blair cleared her throat and asked her own question. "What do *you* think happened, darling?"

Taylor gave it some thought before she spoke, knitting her brows as if to recall the exact sequence of events. "I know everything was okay when we left you at that beach. But when you came back on that other boat, something was different."

Blair nodded. "That was pretty much it. We had an argument on the beach, and I decided that we probably shouldn't see Nick anymore."

"What about?" she asked. "I thought you liked each other."

Blair winced at Taylor's persistence. This was every bit as hard as she'd imagined it would be. "We do like each other, Taylor. I don't think our argument has anything to do with that part. But there are some pretty important things that we don't agree on, and we argued about those, more or less," she finished weakly.

"Like what?"

Blair felt as if she were being grilled under bright lights, but tried very hard to appear casual with her answers. No sense in letting Taylor know how deeply she felt about things. Eleven was too young to be exposed to the raw hurt Blair was feeling.

"Well, for one thing, I think he spends too much time working and worrying about small details—the way I used to."

"I think you're probably right about that one," Taylor said, and Blair had to grin at her impudence.

"And Nick thinks I should make a better home for you—preferably in the States—where you can have your own backyard and friends next door." Blair held her breath now, afraid that Taylor might agree.

"Ugh!" Taylor heaved herself off the sofa and rushed across the room to give Blair a giant hug. "It might be okay for some kids, but I like it here," she said, burying her head in Blair's shoulder.

"'Here' as in Bruges?" Blair pressed, holding Taylor with one arm and smoothing her hair away from her face with her free hand.

"No, silly!" Taylor said. "'Here' as in with you. I love you, Mom."

"I love you, too, darling." And she sniffed back the tears that were threatening to fall.

"Nick's wrong, you know," Taylor said, straightening away from the embrace.

"No, Taylor," Blair disagreed. "He's not wrong. What he says makes sense for a lot of people. But not for us."

Taylor thought about it, then asked, "And this is what you fought about?"

"More or less."

"Seems a shame to break up a beautiful relationship over something so silly," Taylor said, shaking her head at the waste of it all.

"Yes, isn't it," Blair agreed softly.

9

"IF YOU LOOK over your left shoulder, you'll get the best view of the Belfry. Those of you wearing tennis shoes will want to climb it . . . all three hundred and sixty-six steps. After riding around in a boat for an hour, I'd think you could afford the exercise, don't you?"

Blair had long since turned off the recorded tourist blurb, realizing from the beginning that this group would appreciate the spontaneity of her own rather garbled version of the sights and sounds of Bruges. The fact that they were all English speaking had a lot to do with her decision.

It was a daring gamble, because steering the twenty-foot craft along the narrow canals was tricky at the best of times, and talking nonstop tended to distract her. But she'd been on the route for a week now and thought she could handle the extra pressure.

She'd thought wrong.

There was only one bridge left to negotiate. It wasn't even a particularly difficult one, arched like the rest, but high enough so as not to entice her passengers to palm the ceiling with their hands as they were passing underneath. It was high enough to allow Blair to stand, a position she preferred as she spoke candidly to her audience. While some of the bridges required she sit—and duck—she had mostly managed to stay on her feet.

She relaxed, feet spread in a good imitation of a sailor's balanced stance, mentally chalking up one more successful circuit. From her position about twenty feet in front of the bridge, she could see through to the docking area where she was headed. It was a beautiful day, and she held the tiller steady as she lifted her face to catch the full force of the sun's rays.

She should have closed her eyes. If she'd done that one simple thing, she wouldn't have seen him.

But with her face lifted to the sun, she couldn't avoid looking at the string of people lounging over the rough-hewn stones that lined the parapet above.

They saw each other at precisely the same moment.

Nick merely let his jaw drop open, a civilized acknowledgement of surprise.

Blair was somewhat less subtle. She ran into the side of the bridge. And the disaster didn't end there. As could be expected, the only person not seated at the time of the collision was tossed out of the boat.

Blair swallowed an unhealthy amount of canal water before she managed to haul herself over the side of the boat. A couple of the male tourists reached down to help her, but most had been too intimidated by her earlier warnings against standing up in the boat. It served her right, she supposed. Antony had warned her about standing up. Checking to see if her audience was more amused than upset by the minor calamity, she gathered her dignity and settled herself in the captain's chair.

"Need a hand, Blair?"

Shaking the water out of her hair, she just sneered at Antony as he pulled up beside her in his own boat.

"It's a good thing I'm the boss around here," he continued as he pulled ahead and dislodged the bow of her boat from the ancient bricks. "I'll bet anyone else would fire you for a stunt like that."

Reaching over to restart the motor, Blair shot him a glance that at once killed and buried, then calmly followed him back to the dock.

She had other things on her mind.

HE WAS WAITING for her. Over at the side, beyond the point where the line formed for the canal excursions, she could see him.

Shivering now, Blair made her way past the well-wishers—passengers who had "thoroughly enjoyed" their tour of the canals of Bruges—and stalked determinedly toward him. It was his fault, she repeated to herself. Her first accident, and it was his fault. Conveniently she forgot the mess she'd gotten into her first day when she tried to pass a slower boat on the wrong side and had ended up tangled in a fisherman's lines. That didn't count. She'd been a novice then.

"You call this staying out of trouble?" he said before she could open her mouth.

Blair flashed back to when she'd first mentioned the odd jobs, surprised he'd remembered her exact words. But she stiffened her spine, ducking the warm feeling that memory had brought with it, and ignored his opening question.

"What are you doing here?" She stood straight and unflinching as he stared back at her with equal intensity.

"You're here," he said simply. "I had to come."

They stood there, facing off as if they were waiting for the first blow to fall, intimate enemies who battled in a world apart from the rest of the people who shifted and moved around them.

Blair didn't notice the cold, although her skin was peppered with goose bumps and an occasional shiver racked her body. That didn't matter now; nothing mattered except Nick.

"It took you long enough," she finally said. Honesty, it seemed, took priority over hurt feelings.

"I know."

"I didn't know until this moment that I wanted you to come," she murmured, aware of the curious ears that bent in their direction.

"Thank you for that," he breathed just milliseconds before bending forward to touch her lips with his. It was brief, this first kiss in nearly two months, but it was a beginning. Nick cleared his throat and raised his head so he could watch her expression. "You didn't have to want me at all."

"Would you leave if I asked you to?"

"No." And he shook his head slowly, aware they were accomplishing more in this single dialogue than they'd done the entire time they'd known each other. "No, I won't leave until I know there's no reason to stay."

"We're different," she said, knowing the problem was still there. They could want each other forever, but reality had to intrude sometime, and they had some major differences to resolve.

"I think we need to forget about that for a while," he said, draping his jacket over her shoulders as he guided her up the steps to the canal bank. "It keeps getting in the way of what we really want. Maybe later we can work through it. But right now, I just need to hold you." And he did the best he could under the circumstances, keeping one arm around her shoulders as he drew her close to his side.

"That's an admirable thing to say, considering how wet I'm getting you," she joked, lifting her dripping blouse away from her body with her fingertips. "Why don't you wait until I've had a hot bath?"

"Why don't I scrub your back?" he countered, chuckling at the rosy flush that covered her cheeks.

"Taylor will be waiting for me," she said. "I pick her up from school at four."

He smiled. "Let me pick her up. I've missed her, too."

Blair didn't think twice. She grabbed his wrist to check the time, then gave him directions to the school. "Be sure to go by the Market on the way home and buy tomatoes and a baguette. I promised her spaghetti for dinner."

She left him standing at the corner, looking once over her shoulder to make sure he was there, then again to see if he was moving yet.

The shiver that climbed her spine and raced through her limbs had nothing to do with the cold.

"Ah . . . ah . . . ahchoo!"

"Serves you right," Nick said, plucking a clean tissue from the box. "Standing up in a moving boat is reckless, not to mention a little stupid."

"Mom doesn't let me say 'stupid,'" Taylor piped up.

"Excuse me," he apologized to the two of them. "I probably meant to say foolish. Or senseless. Idiotic works, too." Handing the tissue to Blair, he retained an air of superiority that was hard to dent.

Blair tried. "And which 'idiotic' person is going to make the spaghetti tonight?"

"I guess it's up to Taylor and me." He sighed, tucking the blanket around Blair's feet before rising to tower over the sofa where she was nestled amid an assortment of blankets and cushions. "In the meantime, you keep drinking that sherry and you'll feel much better in the morning."

"I've never heard of the sherry cure," she said, nevertheless she took another sip from the glass she held. "I thought it was brandy that was good for colds."

"Mom doesn't have any brandy in the house," Taylor said.

"Which is why we're not trying the brandy cure," he explained smoothly, then turned to pull Taylor out of the rocking chair by the fire. "Come on, midget. We've work to do."

Blair sighed contentedly, snuggling under the warm covers, as they left the room. The emptiness of the past few weeks disappeared in the wake of Nick's presence, and she knew better than to deny it.

She loved him. That hadn't changed, no matter how bad their differences were. And now, it seemed, he was trying to give them another chance.

Leaning forward to pour herself another small glass of sherry, she sneezed, and grabbed another tissue. A pity she was coming down with a cold, but worse things had happened. And it gave Taylor a chance to be alone with Nick. It was something she needed, Blair realized. They were good together. Friends, she realized.

He was a good man, Blair admitted, listening to the cooking noises drifting out from the kitchen as they argued over which pots and pans to use . . . and how much wine to add to the sauce. He was a bit stuffy, but a very good man, nonetheless. And the fact that Taylor liked him, and liked him a lot, was a point she couldn't ignore. She trusted Taylor's judgment.

Taking another sip of the heavy wine, she thought about it. It was hard to ignore the possibilities, equally as difficult to open herself to more hurt. But loving sometimes meant someone got hurt along the way, and Blair was willing to take the chance.

Now she had to find out if Nick was here for a visit...or if he had something more permanent in mind.

They hadn't had a chance to talk, not yet. Over the past several weeks since she'd left Erice, Blair had thought of a thousand things she wanted to say to him . . . to hear him say.

She wanted to explain about how she'd known Taylor was safe, that there had never been anything to worry about.

She needed to let him know she understood the guilt he felt . . . she didn't agree with it, but understood it nevertheless.

She wanted to say she loved him . . . and listen to the deep pitch of his voice as he said the same words to her.

She wanted to go to sleep.

THEY FOUND HER quietly snoring and made a pact not to tell her about the snoring part.

"Mom always snores when she's really tired," Taylor whispered as she delicately lifted the sherry glass from Blair's fingers. "But she usually makes it to bed first."

"At least she's dressed for it," he commented, lifting Blair's shoulders so he could put his arm around her. With a little more effort, he pushed a hand under her legs and lifted her from the sofa.

He followed Taylor through the door to her mother's room, enjoying the weight of Blair in his arms as he waited for Taylor to turn back the covers. He laid her limp body against the sheets, wishing he could lie down beside her, knowing now was not the time. Brushing the wisps of hair from her face, he helped Taylor pull the heavy blankets up to her chin.

"Mom isn't used to drinking very much," Taylor explained in the grown-up voice she reserved for teachers. Throwing one final glance at her sleeping mother, she took Nick's hand and led him back to the living room. "I've never seen her do that before."

"I think it's more a case of mixing the antihistamines with alcohol," he said, realizing the young girl was trying to excuse Blair's behavior. "Things have a tendency to get fuzzy if you take both."

"I guess that explains it," Taylor agreed, not a little relieved.

"So I suppose we'll just have to eat the spaghetti all by ourselves," he said.

Taylor brightened considerably. "Yeah! She won't even miss it if we eat her share!"

"WE WENT TO CRETE when we left Erice," Taylor offered, looking uncertainly at Nick as she helped herself to another piece of bread.

"I know," he said after a moment. This wasn't a conversation he intended to have with Taylor, but he wasn't inclined to lie, either. "Maria Elena told me."

"Mom told me what happened," she said.

Nick raised his brows at that. It didn't seem likely that Blair would give Taylor a blow-by-blow account of their afternoon together, but then, mother and daughter were very close. It wouldn't hurt to ask. "Exactly what did she tell you, midget?"

Taylor gave herself a minute to finish chewing, then told him. "Just that you'd argued and it would be better if we left without seeing you again."

He nodded. Trust Blair to reduce such a complicated scene to the basics. "She was pretty much right. We did argue, but it was mostly my fault. And if you'd waited around a few hours, I would have had a chance to tell her about it." He cleared his throat, then took a sip of the wine he'd brought from the Market. "That's why I'm here now. I want to try to put things together again."

Taylor beamed. "That's okay, then. Mom says arguments aren't meant to be permanent things. They just pop up once in a while to remind you that everybody isn't alike."

"So you don't mind if I try to convince your mother that I, er, care for her?" He stumbled a little over that part, trying to remember this was an eleven-year-old with whom he was talking.

She just shook her head and kept on grinning. "I'll even help by making myself scarce tomorrow," she offered.

Nick froze. That was precisely what had happened the last time. Obviously Blair hadn't gone into any detail about their fight. "Not this time, midget. We'll manage just fine with you here."

"You mean you'll kiss her and everything with me here?"

"Probably not. But we'll get some time alone while you're at school, or after you go to bed." It wasn't the ideal situation, but he needed to show Blair...show both of them...that Taylor wasn't a nuisance to be pushed aside whenever he wanted.

"But if I go over to André's house after school, his mom will make cinnamon rolls," Taylor pleaded. "I haven't had any of her cinnamon rolls since last Friday. Please say you'll ask Mom to let me go!"

"Are you saying that because you want to go, or just to give me some time with your mom?"

She giggled. "Both."

BLAIR AWOKE to the mixed aromas of coffee and toasted bread. Raising first one eyelid, then the other, she focused on the tray Taylor was balancing at the bottom of the bed.

"I gotta go to school, Mom."

Blair moved her bleary gaze to the clock and gasped at the time. "Why didn't you wake me?" she asked, throwing the covers aside in an attempt to get up.

"Because you've got a cold, and he said you're supposed to stay in bed today," Taylor said gruffly as she put the tray aside and moved to block her mother from rising.

"He who?" Blair asked, shaking her head in a futile attempt to dislodge the fog from her brain.

"He Nick, of course," Taylor said, pushing Blair back against the pillows. "He said I was to fix your breakfast, and make sure you ate it in bed."

"Did he say I could get up to go to the bathroom?" Blair asked facetiously, not sure she liked being ordered around.

"He didn't mention it," Taylor replied smoothly. "But I can ask him when he gets here."

"Don't you dare!" Blair ordered, then collapsed into the feather pillows, exhausted by her efforts. "And why is he coming here anyway? I can't see him. I'm sick." Not to mention cranky, she thought. She *hated* being sick.

"He's going to walk me to school, of course," Taylor explained, moving the tray to rest on her mother's knees.

The doorbell rang then, and Taylor swiftly kissed Blair on the cheek before she dashed out of the room. "I'm going to André's after school, so I won't be home until dinner," she shouted from the living room just prior to ducking out the door.

Blair considered rushing to the window to shout permission for the side trip to André's, but restrained herself. Sarcasm was ususally wasted on Taylor.

She sneezed, and grabbed a tissue from the box beside her bed. So much for Nick's sherry cure, she thought, then sneezed a second time. The only thing the sherry had done was make her pass out.

Perhaps that hadn't been such a bad thing, she admitted, pulling a piece of toast from under the linen napkin. Her daughter had set the tray with the best linens and china, she noticed, feeling better as she nibbled at the toast. That was typical, she granted. Taylor probably equated eating in bed with special occasions, thus the elegant setting.

Blair took a sip of orange juice, then crunched her way through a second slice of toast, wondering if she should get up and comb her hair or something before Nick returned. But she was too interested in breakfast to take a break yet, so she just lay there and munched, wondering how she knew he'd be coming back.

It made sense, of course. He'd come a long way to see her, although she'd bet her last dollar that business had something to do with his trip. It didn't seem to matter, though. The fact that he was here was enough for now. She pulled the last piece of toast from the plate and slathered strawberry jam over it, savoring the luxury of breakfast in bed.

The coffee wasn't bad, either. Blair had just poured a second cup from the silver pot when she heard a key turn in the outer door. Taylor must have given Nick her key, she mused.

"You'll have to bring your own cup if you want coffee," she shouted as soon as she heard the door close behind him. "They're on the sideboard."

"I've already had enough coffee this morning, thank you," he said from the doorway.

She should have been self-conscious, she thought, but he didn't make her feel that way. Instead she was filled with a delicious warmth that had nothing to do with the pillows and blankets that encircled her. She licked a bread crumb from her lips, very conscious of his gaze as his eyes narrowed to study this tiny movement. It burned her, igniting her senses in a way she hadn't felt since leaving Erice.

It didn't matter that she was a mess and sick and still a little woozy from the medicine, she realized. He could still make her want him.

So this was how she looked in the morning, he thought, moving his gaze over her tousled hair and slightly pink nose. Except for the nose, she didn't look that much different from any other time. He'd been right about her hair, he realized, remembering how it had always made him think she'd just climbed out of bed.

"You have very sexy hair," he said, leaving his post by the door to sit on the edge of the bed. "That's one of the things I liked about you from the beginning."

Blair gulped, no longer in doubt that her hair was in its typical mess. But sexy? She'd never thought of it that way before. "I suppose I should comb it," she mumbled.

"You really think that will help?" he teased, delighted with the grimace of disgust she didn't bother to hide.

"Probably not," she admitted, then buried her nose in her coffee cup. Draining it, even choking down the dregs, gave her the courage to ask the questions she had meant to ask last night. "Did you come to see me for a reason, or are you just passing through?"

"A little of both," he admitted, moving the tray from her lap and setting it on the floor. Taking her hands in his warm grasp, he continued. "I have business in Amsterdam, but I would have come to see you regardless. It just took a few weeks to talk myself into it."

"Why?"

"I was afraid you'd never want to see me again," he said quietly. "And I guess I couldn't blame you. I was pretty disgusted with myself, too. When you left Erice without even saying goodbye, I figured it was probably for the best."

"I didn't leave because of the argument," she said. "Not really."

"It seemed that way at the time," he inserted, not sure where this was leading.

"I know. But stuff like that usually doesn't bother me. People argue all the time. And since I knew where you were coming from, it was pretty easy to overlook it." Nodding in satisfaction at her analysis, she looked up to catch his mystified stare. "And considering it was my daughter you were worried about . . ."

"Worried *and* feeling guilty," he interrupted. "I would have done anything to be alone with you. And when I realized Taylor might be hurt, I was furious with myself." Shaking his head at the memory, he sighed heavily. "And I took it out on you."

"It doesn't matter anymore, Nick. That's not why I left Erice."

His head snapped up and he pinned her to the pillows with an almost angry stare. "So why did you leave, Blair? I thought that afternoon on the beach we shared something special."

"You're right," she admitted, taking easy, shallow breaths in an effort to control her emotions. It wouldn't do to let him know the depths of her true feelings, especially when she knew better than to expect that he could return them. By skimming the surface of the truth, she could hopefully avoid alerting his suspicions. "But at the time, I guess I was just too embarrassed to stick around," she admitted. "After we...well, after we made love, I imagined myself in love with you. But when you got upset about Taylor, it was pretty easy to figure out it was a one-way street. It didn't make sense that you could say all the things you did if you loved me at all."

"And you left because you were embarrassed?" he prodded, masking his own emotions as he sought to discover her reasons for running. She had thought herself in love with him! His heart pounded an erratic rhythm, spurred by the hope her words had encouraged.

"I suppose so. But mostly it was because I'd figured out you could never accept me ... as I am. And once I solved that piece of the puzzle, the other part faded away."

"What part?" he asked, suddenly confused.

"The part about thinking I was in love," she said simply, smiling at him as if to encourage a slow pupil.

"You mean you're not in love with me after all?" Nick could feel the blood drain from his face as he grappled with this new twist. She loved him, she loved him not. Blair wasn't making a lot of sense.

"Doesn't sound like it to me," she said smoothly, avoiding the intense look in his eyes.

The disappointment was crushing, but he was determined she wouldn't see it. The anger, however, was something entirely different. That was building, almost out of control, and this time it was fully directed at Blair. How could she so lightly dismiss something as important as their love?

"So why were you so glad to see me yesterday?'" he bit out, holding a tight leash on his tongue. He wanted to accuse her of being fickle, of lacking depth . . . of anything at all that would wipe that complacent smile from her face.

"Lowered expectations, I guess."

"Excuse me?"

"I missed you. A lot, I suppose," she said, shaking her head as if mystified by the feeling. "Now that I realize I'm not in love with you, I don't expect the moon anymore. I can just be satisfied with seeing you whenever you drop by."

Blair held her breath, sneaking a look at his face to see if her strategy was working. By presenting him with a no-strings proposition, she'd hoped to put him at ease. He didn't love her, and would obviously be uncomfortable seeing her if he thought she felt otherwise.

It was important that she convince him she was just interested in an affair, because it seemed the only door left open to her. Life was so rarely all or nothing, and this was merely another example. If she took the middle road, settled for less, she would end up with something.

If she demanded it all, even allowed herself to hope for it, then she could very easily end up with nothing at all.

"Sex, and nothing else?" he asked baldly. "An affair, you mean?"

He looked as though he was considering it, and Blair felt her heart race at the possibilities. An affair with Nick would never just be sex, but he didn't have to know that. If she was careful and kept her feelings to herself, it would work.

"It's better than fighting about everything," she pointed out. "Reduce things to basics, trash the happy-ever-after routine, and I might find myself very content with seeing you occasionally." So very sophisticated, she thought, wincing at the words that were flowing nonstop out of her mouth. It was amazing how easy it was to say something she didn't believe. Perhaps this was how Nick had felt when they were fighting on the beach.

"What makes you think I came to offer you anything at all?"

Blair's world almost came to a stop. Steeling herself to meet his gaze, she saw she'd been wrong. Terribly, terribly wrong. It took a major effort not to cry out when he released her hands as he withdrew from her, visibly... and emotionally.

"There's that, I suppose," she finally managed to murmur. It had been a pipe dream anyway, and somewhere along the line she'd allowed herself to hope.

That was something she'd told herself not to do: Hope. It always hurt so much when things went wrong.

"Maybe I just wanted to make sure you made it back here okay, and to apologize for ruining your holiday," he ad-libbed. "I sure as hell didn't come all this way for a one-night stand."

Blair lay speechless as he stood and moved the short distance to her bedroom door. There was nothing she could say that would bring him back. She couldn't afford to—not and survive.

"I'm glad I came to see you," he said, clearing his throat as he turned in the doorway to look at her one last time. "I hate loose ends."

"Of course you do," she whispered, but he was already gone. Blair waited until she heard the outer door swing shut, then turned her face into the pillow.

She sobbed, the tiny convulsion bringing with it a rush of tears.

10

THE LATE AFTERNOON found Blair applying cucumber slices to her swollen eyelids so that Taylor wouldn't notice any evidence of her crying binge.

"What's wrong with your eyes, Mom?" Taylor asked, tossing her book bag onto the foot of the bed.

Blair sighed. So much for the cucumber. "I've got a cold, sweetheart. Remember?"

"Yeah," Taylor said, leaning forward to pull a couple of grapes from the bowl on Blair's lap. "And you still look like you've been crying. What's wrong? Did you and Nick argue again?"

"Not really, Taylor." She popped another grape into her mouth and chewed slowly. Taylor liked Nick, and Blair wasn't sure how to tell her they'd not be seeing him again. "We just talked and realized it wasn't going to work between us."

"Then why is he waiting for me to leave so you can have dinner with him?"

"What?" Blair shot up from the pillows, her eyes darting around the room on the off chance he'd snuck in while she was blinded by the cucumbers. But he wasn't there, and she pinned Taylor with an anxious gaze. "Where?"

"Downstairs," Taylor said nonchalantly, snagging another grape before she got up from the bed. "He's walking me back to André's as soon as I get permission. I'm going to have dinner over there."

"Over where?" Blair was having trouble keeping up.

"At André's, Mom," Taylor repeated patiently. "Why don't you just say yes so you can get busy."

"Doing what?" Taylor was going to André's for dinner, and Nick was coming here. The facts were all there, but the fog in her brain was still too thick for her to make sense out of anything.

"Well, I hate to mention it, but your hair's a mess. More than usual, I mean," Taylor said. "And you might want to wash your face or something. You look like you've been lying in bed crying all day."

"What makes you think I care what I look like?" she grumbled, alarm racing through her as she wondered why Nick wanted to see her. Hadn't they pretty much said it all that morning?

"If you didn't care, you wouldn't have bothered with those cucumbers," Taylor said logically, pointing to slices in the bowl at her elbow.

"That was for your benefit," Blair protested, tucking the bowl under a sheet. "I had no idea Nick would come back."

"Look, Mom. I don't know what the problem is this time, but he's here now and it's your big chance. Don't blow it." And then, almost as if she found the words hard to say, she added hesitantly. "And if you won't be nice to him for your own reasons, then do it for me. I think he's pretty terrific."

"That's blackmail," Blair accused, sliding out of the bed to open a bureau drawer.

"Whatever it takes," Taylor said simply, shrugging off the complaint. "But don't pretend you don't want to see him, 'cause I know better."

"How do you know that?" Blair asked, poking through the silk lingerie in her drawer until she found what she was looking for.

"If you *really* didn't want to see him, you wouldn't be trying to figure out what to wear."

Caught with the evidence between her fingers, Blair conceded the point and returned to sit beside Taylor on the bed. "Have you always been this smart?" she asked.

"Always."

Taylor leaned forward to give her mother a hug, then bounced off the bed. "I won't be gone late," she said, shrugging into her jacket as she headed for the door.

"Call and I'll come walk you home," Blair instructed, unsure when she'd given permission for Taylor to go.

"André's sister will do it," Taylor threw back over her shoulder. Then she paused in the doorway and turned for a parting shot. "Don't forget your hair, Mom. And your face."

Blair heaved a small cushion after the retreating girl, grinning at her sassy manner. Taylor would never say something unkind, but the truth was another matter!

Checking the time on the bedside clock, Blair figured she had ten minutes to make herself presentable. And if what Taylor had said was true, she couldn't afford to waste a single second. Tossing aside the silk camisole she'd found in the drawer, she pulled the flannel nightgown over her head and streaked toward the bathroom.

IT WAS PRECISELY twelve minutes before the doorbell rang.

Blair blew her nose and then brushed it lightly with powder. The result was strictly temporary, she admitted, smoothing her palms over the soft lamb's-wool sweater she'd pulled on over a pair of slacks. The peach tones of the fabrics lent her a false glow of health, and she was pleased with the result.

The bell rang again and she rushed to answer it. The knot in her stomach doubled as she swung the door back, catching Nick in the process of inserting his—or Taylor's—key into the lock.

"Hello, Blair."

His voice rumbled, reaching her with an intensity that made her tremble. It was always this way with him, she thought. It didn't matter that she'd spent the day mourning his departure. That part was forgotten. He was back, and she wanted him to stay.

"Hello, Nick," she whispered. But she couldn't say anything else because all her questions had vanished at the first sight of him.

They stared at each other for long moments without speaking, almost as if they were measuring the emotional distance between them. Then a spark of something flashed in his eyes, and he broke the spell.

"When you didn't come to the door, I thought perhaps you'd fallen asleep," he said, slipping the key into his pocket. Moving forward, he dropped a light kiss on her forehead before steering her back into the room. "I'll just put these things in the kitchen." Lifting the grocery bag to show her the food inside, he then nudged her toward the sofa. "Why don't you sit down. You look a little rocky."

Blair did as he suggested. He was right—she felt more than a little off balance. But it had nothing to do with her cold. She curled up at the end of the sofa, anxious for him to return.

It wasn't a long wait.

He started talking the moment he came back through the kitchen door. "I thought we could spend some nonbelligerent time together," he said, handing her the glass of juice he'd poured in the kitchen. Taking a sip from his own glass, he sat at the other end of the sofa and turned to face her.

"Excuse me?" Blair had expected some sort of explanation, but this wasn't it. *Nonbelligerent?* She took a sip from the glass, then another when she noticed her taste buds were recovering nicely.

He smiled indulgently. "It seems lately we're either making love or fighting. And since you're probably too sick to make love, I thought we could spend an evening just talking."

Blair choked on her juice and amid the subsequent coughing and sputtering, she stole brief, almost furtive glances at the man sitting calmly just a few feet away. *Too sick to make love?* She choked again, grabbing a tissue just in time to sneeze.

"What do you mean 'lately?'" she finally managed. "We haven't made love in nearly two months."

And she'd missed it. Oh, how she'd missed it! Feeling the power of his body inside hers, the breathtaking excitement as he carried her to the stars and beyond . . .

"Which reminds me," he said smoothly. "Are you pregnant?"

She choked again. This wasn't the Nick she remembered. *That* Nick had been a whole lot more subtle. Blair did a quick inventory, checking individual features against the image stored in her memory. It all fit, right down to the faint mole at the tip of his left eyebrow. She remembered the first time she'd noticed it, flushing as she recalled the hot passion of that first kiss.

"Well, are you?" he pressed, brows suddenly drawing together when she didn't answer. Was this why she'd been so touchy?

"Am I what?" she breathed, caught between reliving that first kiss and wanting another. It would be so simple, she thought. Just lean forward, go to him, touch him. It could happen again.

"Pregnant!" he shouted, startling Blair out of her dreams.

She shook her head angrily, denying the notion. "Not because we didn't try," she snapped back. "You didn't seem to care what happened one way or the other at the time." Swinging her hand in a wide arc that was meant to emphasize her point, she sloshed juice onto the sofa. She brushed away the drops from the resilient fabric with fingers that trembled ever so slightly.

"Don't snipe, love," he cautioned. "I don't want to argue with you. Not tonight." He spoke firmly, hiding his disappointment behind the warning. She wasn't pregnant. A pity, he thought. That might have made things easier.

"Don't use that word around me!" she blurted, plunking her glass onto the table before she could spill any more.

"What word?" he asked, mystified. "Snipe? Argue? Pregnant?"

"Love!" she cried. "Love! If you don't mean it, don't use it!"

The light finally dawned. So touchy...and so defensive. Love, he mused. Perhaps it wasn't such a wild dream after all.

"What makes you think I don't mean it?"

"Oh, Nick," she wailed. "We're doing it again." And she jumped up from the couch to cross over to the window. Looking at the quiet canal that ran alongside the foundation of the house, she wondered if life had ever been as complicated as it was now.

"No, we're not," he said easily, his smile gentling her raw nerves. "Close, but not quite an argument."

"How can you tell the difference?"

She turned from the window then, her hair catching the last rays of the day's sunshine and translating them into a halo of light. Moved by her delicate features, Nick found himself on his feet, walking toward her.

He was close, almost too close. He wanted to touch her, to forget the words and drag her into his arms. But he waited, just a moment, because he wanted her to know why.

"This isn't an argument, because I don't want to leave and you don't want to throw me out."

"How do you know I don't want to throw you out?" she breathed. It was here again, the excitement, the thrills. It paralyzed her, and left her defenseless against the need it created. This was the man she'd loved on that hot Sicilian beach, and it no longer mattered that he didn't love her in return.

It hurt, but it didn't matter. Not now, when he was so close.

"Because I'm holding you," he said softly, resting his hands on her hips, pulling her forward until their bodies were lightly touching. "And you're holding me back."

It happened as he spoke, her arms lifting to rest on his shoulders, her face tilting up for his kiss. It was where she wanted to be, in his arms, her mouth enjoying their first real kiss in weeks.

His hunger showed.

Threading his fingers through the tangled curls at her neck, he held her steady as his tongue thrust deep inside her mouth. He pushed into her hot sweetness and relearned the taste of her. He swallowed her cries and reveled at the way she pulled him closer, opening herself to his kiss, giving everything without a thought of holding back.

This was what had brought him back. All the words and arguments and differences aside, they still had this.

It was something to build on.

His mouth became less demanding, gentler. The initial greed had been satisfied, and now he was content to trail soft kisses across her face. He touched her eyelids with his lips, then drew back to watch as they fluttered open. In the window's light, he noticed for the first time the slight puffiness that rimmed her lids. He chastised himself for having forgotten she was ill.

Around Blair, it was remarkably difficult to think straight.

"I think we should do something about dinner," he murmured, dropping a kiss on the tip of her nose before taking a step backward.

"Dinner?" she breathed, her hands dropping to her sides. Holding him made her forget everything, dinner and her cold included.

"Yes, dinner." He grinned. "As in nutrition. You're still sick, remember?"

"If this is anything like the sherry cure, I don't think I want any," she grumbled, not terribly happy at the practical direction events were taking.

"Are you always this cross when you get sick?" he asked, snagging a soft blanket from the sofa and draping it around her shoulders.

"Probably," she said, then promptly sneezed. "But if you think I'm bad, you should try being around Taylor. She's an absolute terror when she has to stay in bed."

"And we all know who she inherited that trait from," he commented dryly, tugging her hand as he drew her across the room. Tucking the box of tissues under her arm and holding the blanket with her free hand, she followed him into the kitchen.

There was a high stool on the far side of the work-table, and she settled herself there as Nick retraced their steps to the living room and retrieved their juice.

He leaned back against the counter and took a long sip from his glass. "I have to go to Amsterdam in the morning," he said. "That's why I came back tonight. I didn't want to leave without seeing you again."

Blair swallowed, wishing she could think of some-thing besides how much she was going to miss him when he was gone. Since leaving Erice, she had tried to put him out of her mind. That had been the only ap-proach open to her, knowing she would never see him again.

But the loving hadn't stopped just because she'd wanted it to. There had been so many nights that she'd dreamed he was beside her, sharing her life, her love. Dreams, she told herself, weren't meant to last.

And now that she'd seen him again, kissed him, she knew she would never forget. She loved him, but this time there could be no fantasy that he loved her back.

"I was hoping that I could come back here after the meetings in Holland," he said slowly, feeling his way through her silence. "I have a couple of free days be-fore I have to get back to the office . . . and I don't know anyone in Amsterdam."

Nick kept his words even, holding back the fear that she would say no, his breath caught high in his throat.

He wouldn't have dared to hope before, but her kiss had held more than passion. It had been so sweetly loving . . . giving . . . that it had shaken his soul.

But he knew better than to believe everything could be solved with a kiss. There were problems to resolve, nothing insurmountable, but nevertheless there were barriers between them.

Nick was working his way through some of them, and now he just needed to convince Blair she wanted to help him. Changes needed to be made, and they couldn't be completely one-sided.

"I thought you weren't interested in an affair," she said slowly. It didn't make sense, not after he'd seemed so outraged by the idea that morning. And she had to know where to draw the line, just how far she could let her dreams stray.

"I'm not," he said clearly. "And I'm betting everything that you're not, either."

Nick rounded the corner of the worktable and came to stand beside her, lifting her chin as he dared her to be honest. "I came back tonight hoping you really didn't mean what you said this morning. I thought about it all day, and the only thing that makes sense is that you love me. Maybe only a little, but it's there and you're hiding it."

"What makes you think that?" she whispered.

"Because I'm in love with you, and the woman I know...the woman I *love*...wouldn't have made such a cold-blooded proposition."

A tiny cry escaped her lips, and with it the hurt and pain vanished. Blair trembled, her eyelids drifting closed over eyes that were suddenly filled with tears. He loved her, and was strong enough to admit it.

"Why didn't you say that this morning?" she asked quietly, opening her eyes to find his lips just a breath away.

He had to kiss her first, holding her lips under his own as he sealed their intimate bargain. But he kept the touch light, drawing away when she pressed him for more. Nick moved back to the cooking side of the worktable before answering.

"Things got out of hand, and it didn't occur to me then that you were just talking through your hat." He smiled, filling her with a glorious sense of wonder as he repeated those magic words. "I love you. I knew that this morning, but that muddled line of garbage you were feeding me threw me off."

"It was designed to," she admitted, smirking at his astonishment. "The last thing I wanted was for you to believe I still loved you. I was afraid that would scare you off, and I decided part of you was better than nothing at all."

"So do you?" he asked quietly, holding her gaze as he pressed for an answer. "Do you love me?"

"Of course, I do!"

He let it out then, a sigh that passed through his lips and took with it the pressures of not knowing, the frightening possibility that he'd been wrong. Steadying himself with palms flattened on the counter, he took several deep breaths before he could speak.

"You could have said that five minutes ago," he finally managed to say, dragging open a nearby drawer in search of utensils. He found the knife he'd been looking for and held it up expectantly as he waited to hear the words.

"I love you," she obliged. She liked the way it felt on her lips so much that she said it again. "I love you." And then she raised an eyebrow at the knife that Nick still held up in the air. She was sure he didn't even notice, but anyone else would have thought it was a bit odd.

"Good." It wasn't much of a comment, but he had other things on his mind. And saying any of them was out of the question, especially now. Blair wasn't ready yet for talk of marriage. And children . . . he wondered how she felt about having more children. Suddenly he noticed the knife in his hand and wondered what he was doing holding it up like that. Setting it carefully on the counter, he reached into the grocery bag and pulled out the makings for a salad and proceeded to clean and chop.

Blair watched for five minutes, then couldn't stand it any longer. "So what do we do now?"

Nick didn't pause in his chopping. "Nothing. Except eat dinner, that is. We're having my world-famous onion soup," he said, grinning when he looked up to see her licking her lips. "But that's probably an hour away, so you'll have to make do with a salad until it's ready."

"Onion soup in an hour?" she asked, disbelief written all over her face. "That's not even half cooked!"

"You'll eat it and love it," he threatened. "Your taste buds won't know the difference. I know you should have chicken soup, but I couldn't bring myself to buy one of those things in the Market."

She nodded. "With the head on, you mean."

"Precisely." He shuddered.

"What do you mean, we do nothing?" she finally asked, getting back to the original subject. "You'd think we should celebrate or something."

"Or even consummate," he teased, pretending not to notice that Blair was blushing furiously, just as he'd intended, and couldn't even think of a comeback.

He spent another few minutes organizing the soup on the stove before getting back to the subject. "We'll celebrate when you're better," he said firmly. "And in the meantime, we're going to avoid talking about it, too. There are still a lot of problems ahead of us, and I'd rather put them aside for a while."

"Isn't that like running away from them?" she asked.

But Nick shook his head as he reached into the cabinet above the counter and pulled out two plates. Heaping salad on them, he grabbed forks and led the way to the table. "I just think we need to work on the positive things first. Then maybe the rest of the stuff will be easier to resolve."

It was logical, she thought, sinking into the chair Nick held for her.

So why did she have the feeling it could never be that easy?

11

H<small>E HEARD HER</small> before he saw her.

She was laughing, and he followed the sound until his eyes picked her out of the crowd. Her laughter rang out again, and she reached up to the very top vase to pull out a single violet bloom.

Blair was surrounded by flowers, and was apparently selling them. Nick moved a few feet to the side to watch as she carefully wrapped the chosen blossoms in paper and handed the bundle to a young boy. He said something to her, and she laughed again before solemnly accepting the coins he handed her.

Nick waited just a few moments longer, then approached the flower kiosk. "Your landlady said you'd be here, but she didn't mention anything about selling flowers."

Blair spun around, her eyes sparkling with excitement. "You're back!" And she leaned across the counter, her face lifted for a kiss. Nick obliged with a chaste peck, mostly because there were too many people milling around to do much else.

That could come later.

"I thought you wouldn't be here until later this afternoon," she murmured, fidgeting with some flowers that stood in a vase on the counter between them.

"I hopped on an early plane," he said, catching her gaze and holding it. "I couldn't wait any longer to see you."

It had been two days since he'd left for Amsterdam, almost an eternity. Blair felt herself drowning in the dark pools of his eyes, and shut hers against the sensation. It was too much, she thought. Too fast.

And it wasn't as if they had any privacy! "I'm glad you came early," she said. "I'll get Leo to take over and we can go for lunch."

"You don't have to stay all day?"

"I hadn't planned to," she said, shaking her head at the notion. "I just help out when I can't find anything else to do. I also work at the T-shirt shop," she said, pointing vaguely toward a narrow street. "Leo's brother owns that, but I like it here better. Especially on gorgeous days like this."

"What about the canal excursions?" he asked, grateful she wasn't doing that again today.

"That was just temporary," she replied, scanning the crowd in front of a nearby shop. "I probably won't do it again unless they need help on a busy day."

Nick silently prayed the boss would think twice before asking Blair to help out, but kept his thoughts to himself. If Blair set her mind to doing something, all the arguments in the world wouldn't convince her otherwise.

A customer claimed her attention, and Nick stepped back a few feet, letting his gaze drift over the scene in the Market—the center of the old city that was surrounded by ancient historic buildings. The square itself was filled with people—mostly tourists, he guessed—who wandered past the numerous kiosks that were scattered across the cobblestones.

Horse-drawn carriages passed by, also filled with tourists. Nick watched as a young girl ran alongside one of the carts, offering flowers as she kept pace with the horse's gait. At a signal from the people in the carriage, the driver pulled up and the flowers were exchanged for a few coins.

Shoving the money into a pocket, the girl turned and Nick realized it was Taylor. He counted to ten, keeping a rein on his tongue as he mentally listed and rejected at least a dozen reasons why Taylor was hawking flowers on the street. Nothing made sense, and the combination of Blair in the kiosk and Taylor pushing posies on the street made him wonder if money was a problem. The fact that it was a school day only deepened his concern.

"Nick!" Taylor had finally spotted him, and she ran the last few steps before throwing herself into his open arms. He hugged her tightly enough to make her squeal before he set her back on her feet.

"I thought Mom said you wouldn't be here until later!" she accused, grabbing his hand to lead him back toward the kiosk. "She's got a terrific dinner planned and we're going to put all the good stuff on the table so it looks really romantic and everything," she enthused, not in the least concerned that she was giving the surprise away. "And I get to help with the dessert!"

"Precisely what do you get to do with the dessert that makes it so special?" he asked, wondering how Blair planned on turning dinner for three into a romantic interlude.

"Now that would be telling!" Taylor said, wagging a finger at his indelicate question. "You'll just have to wait and see. Hey, Mom, did you see who's here?"

Blair pressed a bouquet into an elderly lady's hand before turning to smile fondly at her daughter. "I saw and I'm trying to find Leo so I can do something about it," she said.

"I'll find him," Taylor offered, handing over the coins she'd pulled out of her pocket. "I'm out of flowers anyway." She dashed off across the plaza, zigzagging among the clusters of tourists and other obstacles.

"How long do you get for lunch?" Nick asked, counting the minutes they could spend together before she had to get back to work.

"Oh, I won't work anymore today," she said. "I was just doing Leo a favor anyway. He really didn't ask me to stay more than a couple of hours in the first place."

Not much of a job, he thought, wondering if she'd been counting on the money. But Blair didn't appear concerned, so he let it go . . . for the moment. "And Taylor, can she come with us?"

Blair shook her head. "She has classes this afternoon. And I think she said something about André bringing a lunch for the two of them."

Taylor burst through the crowd then with an almost breathless man in tow. He was wearing a T-shirt that read I LOVE BRUGES and a baseball cap promoting the Chicago Bears. Blair performed the introductions, kissed Leo on the cheek and promised to come back and help another day. "Especially nice days like this," she said, grinning when Leo pushed a bunch of flowers into her hands.

The trio sauntered across the plaza toward the post office, where Taylor spotted André waiting for her. She waved wildly in his direction, kissed her mother on the cheek and looked up at Nick. "Are you going to pick me up after school?"

"I can."

"Great!" She hugged Nick swiftly around the middle before he could bend down. "If Mom doesn't care, I'll take you to my most favorite place in Bruges."

"That's a deal," he agreed, wondering what he was getting himself into when he heard Blair's chuckle.

"Wear tennis shoes," Taylor warned. And then she was off to join André and they disappeared into a narrow side street.

"Something tells me I'm going to need a big lunch," he said, slipping his fingers through Blair's.

"A stiff drink wouldn't hurt, either," she suggested, then led the way toward the restaurant.

It wasn't until they'd eaten their way through sautéed prawns and scallops that he finally asked her about the flowers.

"I told you about that," she said lightly. "I just help out when there isn't anything else going on."

"I can't imagine you earn enough to make it worth your while," he said, leaning back in his chair so the waitress could take his plate.

"That depends on what you think is enough," she teased, pinching off a bloom from the bouquet and lifting it to her nose. She sniffed delicately, then tucked the stem behind her ear. "I happen to think a bouquet is a perfectly lovely thank-you, don't you?"

"That's all he gave you . . . a bouquet?"

"What else did you expect?" she asked.

"Hard cash might do you more good," he growled, wondering how Blair could support herself if she couldn't even find a job that paid real money.

"What makes you think I need cash?" Her brows knitted together as she stared across the table at him. "Do I look like I'm penniless?"

Nick took a long swallow of beer from his glass and set it down precisely at the center of the cardboard coaster. "No, but when I saw Taylor selling flowers on the street, I figured things were kind of tight and she was helping out."

Blair laughed then, delighted with the embarrassed flush on his face. Nick really thought she had a money problem, she realized, trying to stifle her amusement. But then Blair remembered she'd purposely left him in the dark as to her financial situation. This was probably a good time to set him straight.

"I'm not nearly as irresponsible as you seem to think, Nick," she said, patting his hand with the tips of her fingers in a soothing gesture. "And I guess this misguided conclusion of yours is partially my fault."

"At least," he growled, then waited for the rest.

"I had a lot of money put away when Taylor and I left the States, mostly from a couple of lucky investments I'd made, the rest from the sale of our house. My parents left it to me when they died—I guess that was about ten years ago now—and with the real-estate market going like it has . . ." She realized Nick knew enough about finances to figure that one out for himself. "And as far as Taylor's future is concerned, there's a nice trust fund her father set up for her that we've never even touched."

"You've never talked about him before," he said, suddenly aware she had shared more of her personal life in the past few minutes than she'd done in all their time together.

"There's not much to say," she said, shrugging off the subject as though it lacked any great importance. "Taylor has never seen him. I'm not even sure if he knows whether she's a boy or a girl."

"You mean he divorced you while you were pregnant?" Nick was stunned, incapable of believing a man could treat his wife so cruelly.

Blair sighed, wishing Nick wouldn't take all this so seriously. It had all happened such a long time ago, and even then things hadn't been that bad. Nick would have problems understanding, she knew, but something told her the whole truth just might make sense to him . . . eventually.

"Getting married was the one mistake we didn't make," she finally said. "By the time I discovered I was pregnant, we had already gone our separate ways. But we had parted friends, so I decided the least I could do was tell him about the baby."

"And he didn't offer to marry you?"

"Of course he did," she said, shaking her head at his assumption. "But Larry didn't love me, and I wasn't in love with him, so of course I turned him down."

"I'll bet he was relieved," Nick ground out.

"No, I really think he liked the idea of a baby. But I knew his parents were thrilled when I said no. I'm sure they thought I was after his money." Blair shuddered at the close call, remembering how grateful she'd been to realize his parents would never be her in-laws.

"Anyway, Larry and I basically parted ways and I never expected to hear from him again. He must have read the birth announcement in the paper, though, because after Taylor was born, he sent a lawyer over to explain about the trust fund."

"You took it?"

"Of course, I took it. It's Taylor's money, and if she wants to use it someday, it will be there. And if she doesn't, she can give it back to Larry, or whatever."

The waiter moved in then, serving tiny cups of espresso alongside an assortment of chocolate petit fours. Blair wondered if Nick was going to pursue the thing about Taylor's father. She hoped not, mostly because she had other things on her mind—such as what they were going to do with the rest of the afternoon.

"How does she feel about not having a father?"

"You really want it all, don't you?" Blair sighed, taking a sip of coffee.

"Yes. These are pretty basic things."

"Aren't you afraid we'll start arguing again?"

"Not unless you start it," he said. "I'm just trying to get to know more about you. And Taylor. She's part of this, too."

"I told her the whole story a few years back. About how he'd offered to marry me, and about the money. She felt pretty good about that, mostly because she'd always thought he hadn't cared enough to stick around when I got pregnant. Now she realizes he's a good man in his own way and that we probably made the best decision for all of us."

"That's a pretty mature attitude," he said, draining his coffee and pushing the saucer aside.

"I've got a pretty mature daughter," Blair agreed. "She could have tried out all sorts of tantrums and such, but I guess she realizes things have worked out okay the way they are."

Nick put some bills beside the lunch tab and picked up the bouquet to hand to Blair. "We'd better get these into water," he suggested, rising from his chair.

They joined the pedestrian traffic that eventually dispersed into the Market, then drifted along the canal that verged on the house where Blair's flat was situated. They were content to walk and enjoy the sunshine, and were nearly home before Nick brought up the subject again.

"So Taylor was selling flowers because . . . ?" he began, then looked sideways at Blair for the answer.

"Because she had the morning off from school and likes practicing languages on the tourists."

"And you were in the kiosk . . . ?"

"Because I think it's fun."

"Like driving a boat?" he pressed, finally getting into the swing of things.

"Absolutely," she agreed, digging in her pocket for the house key.

"Do I want to know about the other 'jobs' you take?"

"Probably not," she said sweetly, turning away before he could see the smile of success on her face. It was lovely having Nick understand her life, and even better when there were no more secrets between them.

They mounted the three steps to the front door, and Nick reached around in front of her to push it open. She lifted her face to smile her thanks, and found her lips just inches from his.

It was irresistible. He was so close, and she was so incredibly hungry for him. Without any thought for where they were, she rose on her toes and with a hand on his arm for balance, she closed the remaining inches between them.

Their lips touched. It was a gentle beginning, not unlike the first breeze of a spring storm. But she wanted more. Blair lifted herself higher, begging for a firm response, a commitment.

Nick held himself stiffly, waiting for Blair to set the pace. He was almost afraid to join in, knowing a little taste would only whet his appetite for more. He wanted her so badly, standing there, in the open doorway with the breeze of early summer flowing through her hair.

She was so very feminine, he thought, lifting a hand to her hair so he could slide his fingers into the silky waves. So very much a woman.

He heard the tiny cry of frustration as she lifted her arms to lock her hands behind his neck. Nick gave in to her then, largely because there were no other choices. His tongue slashed across her lips, parting them just moments before he thrust into her mouth.

It was hot there. And sweet. Oh, so very, very sweet.

Their tongues danced a slow waltz until he pulled away, breathless with the incredibly erotic movement. He nibbled at her bottom lip, then sucked gently until it was swollen and tender.

Then he kissed her again, swallowing her cries and absorbing her tremors as his arms tightened around her shoulders. He could feel the fullness of her breasts against his chest, remembered from another time how sensitive her nipples could be. He wanted to touch her there, excite her as she was exciting him.

It was magic.

The scent of flowers invaded his nostrils, and Nick inhaled the heady aroma. Flowers, he remembered. Opening his eyes, he found himself staring into the colorful blooms that were clenched in her hand at his neck.

Flowers.

Gently, slowly, Nick drew away, just inches at first, because he found it a very hard thing to do. And then more, because he suddenly remembered where they were.

"The flowers need water," he said softly, a half smile forming on his lips as she looked at him curiously. "The ones in your hand."

"Oh." She seemed incapable of saying anything else, so Nick took charge and pushed her gently through the door. With her lips still shaping the word 'oh', all he could think about was how much he wanted to push his tongue back into her mouth.

He took a step toward her, meaning to do just that, but Blair was already mounting the long flight of stairs to her apartment. Just as well, he decided. He doubted his control would stand much more testing, and making love to Blair on the stairway was out of the question.

Blair inserted the key into the lock and looked back over her shoulder at the man who had followed her so closely up the stairway. "I'll just pop these into water and then we'll find something to do this afternoon," she said, pushing the door open as she spoke.

The telephone began to ring, interrupting what ever she might have said next. Nick followed her inside, pulling the door closed behind him.

Blair went to the telephone and talked for a few moments, motioning Nick toward the sofa. He watched her eyes light up at something that she heard, and could make no sense of her response because he was too busy looking at her. The full skirt she wore had a flower pattern in bold colors, offsetting the sleeveless lace blouse of startling white. The clothes swayed with each movement, with every breath. He watched the rise and fall of her breasts under the blouse, amazed that it was every bit as erotic as seeing her naked under the hot Sicilian sun.

His mind was wandering along those lines when she replaced the receiver. "That was Frankie," she said, pretending to ignore the heated message in his eyes. "He wants me to drive for him tomorrow."

"Drive for him?" Nick wasn't really up to having a conversation, but Blair seemed to want to share this with him.

"The carriage," she explained. "Frankie owns a couple of the horse carriages in the Market. Sometimes I drive for him if there isn't anything else going on."

"Of course, you do," he sighed, wondering how much she knew about horses and whether it mattered. "So are you?"

"I told him I'd stop by and see him later," she said. "I wasn't sure if you were going to be here tomorrow."

"I had planned on it," he said. "But I have to drive in to Brussels in the afternoon. I'd hoped you'd come with me."

"Then I'll tell him no." She grinned, turning on her heel and pushed through the kitchen door.

Nick let his breath leave his body in a slow sigh as he watched her go. When she was out of sight, he sought a measure of control. As much as he wanted to follow her, to hold her, to pull off her clothes and bury himself deep inside her where it was hot and wet and so incredibly tight, he thought he'd better not.

Blair didn't look like she was ready for him, not yet, and he certainly didn't want to make a wrong move. Oh, he knew she wanted him. But it was very likely that she would feel uncomfortable about making love in the afternoon, here, in the apartment she shared with Taylor.

Then again, maybe she wouldn't.

Nick really didn't know what she was thinking, but decided to put his own appetites on hold. Waiting wouldn't hurt, he reminded himself, and they would probably be better off in the long run if they spent the afternoon talking.

Perhaps she'd like a drive in the country. Nick thought about it, then pulled a map from his pocket, spread it on the coffee table in front of the sofa and sat down to study Bruges and the surrounding area. A drive to Zeebrugge would be nice, he thought, listening to the noises from the kitchen as she ran water into a container.

Five minutes later, Nick was still immersed in the map when Blair finally reappeared through the kitchen door. He glanced up at the slight noise the door made as it swung shut behind her, watched as she took a single step into the living room before retreating to lean against the door frame.

She was wearing silk, he noticed. Not the summery skirt and blouse she'd been wearing earlier. Just silk, or something that looked like silk. There wasn't really enough of it to tell for sure, he admitted, especially from his place on the sofa.

But it certainly gave him an excellent perspective on what was beneath it. He swallowed hard, then coughed just enough to clear his throat of whatever was blocking it. "Are you trying to vamp me?"

"Is it working?" Blair asked huskily. She had thought she'd feel ridiculous, but she didn't. The impulse that had made her strip down to her camisole and panties had seemed almost ludicrous at the time.

She was glad she'd given in to it. Surprising Nick was almost as exciting as kissing him.

"Yes, it's working."

"Then I guess I'm vamping." And all nervousness drifted away as she waited for Nick to make the next move.

He took his time, allowing his eyes to reach every inch of her, knowing that in moments his fingers would be sliding along the silky skin that turned to velvet between her legs . . . on the underside of her breasts. His body ached with its own demands, but still he waited.

They had all afternoon.

"Come over here." Suddenly looking wasn't enough. Nick held out a hand in invitation, not moving from his place on the sofa. It didn't make sense to move, he realized. They would just have to come back here where he could lay her down. So he waited.

"Why don't you come over here?" she teased, delighted with the flash of frustration that zipped across his expression.

"Because I thought you'd rather be comfortable the first time," he said silkily, dropping his hand to rest on the back of the sofa. "But if you want it standing up, then I guess you don't have to move at all."

Blair gasped against the hot bolt of wanting that tore through her slender body. The image he had drawn for her was almost too much, and she held his daring gaze as she made a decision.

He didn't blink as she moved toward him. She walked slowly, padding on bare feet until she was just inches from his knees. Their gazes locked, she was unaware he'd moved his hand until it touched her.

His fingers settled lightly on her hip, the silk camisole an erotic barrier between them. She could feel his heat, shivered as he began an easy stroking motion that dragged the silk back and forth over her skin. When the camisole gave way to the callused touch of his fingers, she sank forward, draping herself over his warmth.

Still he caressed her, just there, in that tiny spot around her hip. Her knees fell to either side of his thighs as he half sat, half slouched against the back of the sofa, and she found the position an extremely vulnerable one...and terribly exciting. She was open to him, ready to feel the hard strength of his body against hers, in hers. Blair huddled closer to him, following as he fell back against the cushions, her fingers busy with the buttons of his shirt. She concentrated hard, shuddering when his fingers strayed from her hip to trace the lacy edge of her panties.

He slowed her frantic fingers, not because he wasn't anxious, but because he didn't want to hurry.

He'd learned the first time with Blair how incredibly exciting she could be if he took his time. Hot and fast had its place, he knew, but right now, with her trembling body draped across his, he wanted her to wait for it.

"Put your hands on my shoulders," he urged her, grasping her wrists to move them away from the buttons.

She did as he asked, opening her lips to his demanding mouth. He held back nothing this time. Not like before, downstairs. He thrust into her again and again, drinking her sweet moans as his tongue delved deeper and deeper.

She felt his hands holding her at her waist, trembled when he lifted her camisole until her breasts were uncovered. When he dragged his lips from her mouth, she cried out, then she cried again when they closed around a hard, throbbing nipple. His fingers moved between her legs, caressing her through the silk barrier, lightly at first, then harder when she moved against him.

She loved him with her mouth. Bracing herself against the sofa with her forearms, Blair dropped wet kisses on his forehead, leaned down to dip her tongue into his ear. She wanted more of him, but he refused to release her breast, and she threw her head back in surrender to the demands. Her hair floated down her back, lightly brushing the sensitive skin as she swayed to his rhythm.

It was so intense, the way he loved her. He made her feel so incredibly alive!

Slowly, he remembered thinking. But it suddenly made no sense. His fingers left her hot center and wrapped around the bits of silk at her hips, tugging until they split away under the pressure. His lips sought her other breast, and he pulled her into his mouth, consumed by the need to take everything she had to offer.

He allowed her to help then, pulled at the clothes she loosened until he was naked against her. She raised her hands to pull off the camisole, the last thing between them, but he stopped her, murmuring hot, sensual words that made her forget anything and everything except what he was doing to her with his mouth, his hands.

Blair thought she recognized the stars that burst in flashes of blinding light as she followed him through a galaxy of adventures, her body arching to his caress, her heart racing in a frantic beat.

And when they became one, when he joined them in the ultimate embrace, Blair cried out at the beauty of it all.

This was new, more exciting than the last time, almost another dimension in the intimacy of lovemaking. Because she loved him, and he loved her, it now became something infinitely precious.

With strength and tenderness, Nick carried them up to meet those stars, watching the face of the woman he loved as she became lost in the glorious rhythm. Then he shut his eyes to reality and let his body lead the way, knowing his heart was safely in her care.

BLAIR GRINNED at the picture they made. Taylor was jumping up and down with the boundless energy of youth, and Nick was nearly reduced to crawling through the open door behind her.

"He did it, Mom!" Taylor exclaimed, bouncing over to kiss Blair before returning to hurry Nick along. "All three hundred and sixty-six steps!"

Nick went straight to the sink and poured himself a tall glass of water, drinking it straight down before refilling the glass. When he thought he'd satisfied his thirst, he turned back to Blair and Taylor, wincing at the energy emanating from the young girl.

"You could have warned me." His aggressive tone should have cautioned her, but Blair figured he'd be getting even with her somehow and saved her sympathy for herself.

"About the Belfry?" she asked innocently, reaching past him to turn off the running water.

"Yes, Blair," he said gruffly. "About the Belfry. You knew that was where she was taking me."

"I thought you had energy to burn," she countered, remembering how she'd had to convince him to get dressed in time to collect Taylor from school. It hadn't been easy, especially since they'd been in the middle of some very serious lovemaking when she'd noticed the time on the clock. He'd grumbled, but when she'd pushed him out of the bed, he'd complied.

"You should have worn tennis shoes like I told you," Taylor said, selecting an apple from the bowl on the counter. "You probably wouldn't have slipped so much then."

Blair chuckled and turned to stir something on the stove as Nick mumbled something about not bringing tennis shoes along. Poor Nick, she thought, lifting the spoon to taste the thickening sauce. It was just about right, she decided, turning the gas flame low to allow it to simmer.

When Nick leaned over her shoulder to check out the contents of the various pots and pans, Blair remembered dinner was supposed to have been a surprise. With mock gruffness, she pushed him away from the stove and out of the kitchen. "You're due back at seven. Don't be late."

"And bring some flowers," Taylor suggested. "I don't think Mom got these into water soon enough," she said, showing Nick the vase holding the wilted bouquet.

"Shame on you, Taylor," Blair chastised, blushing at her daughter's sharp eye for detail. While she'd managed to fill the vase with water, Blair had somehow forgotten to add the flowers. Strange how some things escaped her when Nick was around. "You never ask a man to bring you flowers."

"I didn't ask Nick to bring me flowers," she countered. "I asked him to bring *you* flowers. There's a difference."

"Maybe Leo will have something nice," was all Nick could manage before dropping a kiss on Blair's upturned face and darting out the door.

Blair laughed. She hadn't realized he had enough energy left to move that fast.

"I'M GOING to take a shower," Blair said sometime later, shutting off the stove as she replaced the lid on the steaming pan.

"What about dessert?"

"We'll practice lighting the brandy after my shower," Blair said, referring to the flaming treat she'd concocted. She had promised Taylor she could serve it, and she wanted to make sure the young girl knew just how much brandy to use in order to achieve the proper effect.

"Have you changed your mind about letting me light it?" Taylor asked hopefully.

"Absolutely not," Blair retorted. "Matches are dangerous. We'll let Nick do that part."

She patted Taylor on the shoulder and headed back toward her room, thinking about the lilac-scented soap she'd bought and wondering whether Nick would even notice.

12

SHE HEARD the screaming first.

Blair slammed off the water just in time to hear the pounding of Taylor's feet across the hardwood floor of her bedroom. She was still screaming, and Blair stumbled out of the shower stall and across the bathroom, yanking a towel from the bar as she threw open the door.

Taylor skidded to a stop, then grabbed Blair's hand and began pulling. "It's a fire, Mom!" she screamed again, the tears streaming down her face as she led the way through the bedroom. "I started a fire and I can't get it to go out!"

Blair's heart thudded in stark fear. Fire! She could smell it now, could see the thick smoke curling through her bedroom door. She jerked Taylor to a stop and swung the young girl around to face her.

"Where's the fire, Taylor? Your room, the kitchen? Where?!" Blair didn't want to go into the living room if it was already burning in there, and was mentally running over the escape route from her bedroom window.

"In the kitchen," Taylor sobbed, then tried to run in that direction. "It's the furnace, and it's all my fault!" she wailed, frustrated with her attempts to get back there.

Blair wasn't about to let Taylor go back. "Now listen hard, Taylor. I need you to go to Mrs. Rabineau's and tell her to call the fire department. Then get everyone out of the house and stay out." Blair grabbed a robe and pulled it on, dragging Taylor out toward the living room as she spoke. "And that means you, too!"

She pushed Taylor toward the front door and turned her attention to the dark cloud of smoke that billowed from the kitchen. Even with the door open, she couldn't see much except smoke. Taking it as a good sign there were no flames, Blair took a deep breath and plunged into the swirling cloud.

She made herself take her time, watching carefully for flames or flying sparks. Most of the noise seemed to be originating from the furnace, so she took a chance and skidded over to the sink and dived underneath it to retrieve the fire extinguisher.

It took a lifetime to figure out how it worked, or it seemed like it at the time. She cursed her shaking fingers, and finally pulled out the pin. The crackling noise was getting louder, and she didn't dare get any closer to the source. She could feel the scorching heat where she stood, and knew better than to move toward it.

Blair took a deep breath to steady her aim, then coughed out the smoke as she raised the extinguisher and pushed the button.

White foam shot through the smoke and sizzled as it made contact with the burning coal. She held the extinguisher high, aiming it in the general direction of the furnace, hoping the fire hadn't spread. It was only a small extinguisher, and she could feel it emptying rapidly. She couldn't see anything now, but the crackling noises were beginning to dissipate.

The extinguisher fizzled, leaving her alone with an empty canister and a smoke-filled room. She peered through the smoke, hope surging inside her because she could hear no more crackling noises. Taking a couple of cautious steps forward, she was finally able to see the furnace.

It was still smoking heavily, but there were no flames.

Blair coughed, then coughed again as the smoke finally got to her. She heard the pounding of feet on the stairs, but she stayed where she was.

She didn't want to risk taking her eyes off the furnace, not until someone else took over.

Luckily for Blair, a whole crowd of helpers charged in the door and pulled her out of the smoking room. The smoke had settled in her lungs, and she was coughing uncontrollably when the fireman escorted her down the steps and outside. Once there, someone stuck a mask over her nose and mouth and babbled something totally unintelligible to Blair.

"He says to breathe, Mom," Taylor translated, her small hands clasping her mom's. "You've got smoke in your lungs and you need to breathe the oxygen."

"No kidding," she mumbled, pretty much to herself because no one could possibly understand what she was saying from behind the mask. Blair pulled the plastic mask away to cough up a cloud or two of smoke, taking deep cleansing breaths in between.

"They said you put it out all by yourself, Mom" Taylor supplied, eavesdropping on the conversation a couple of the men were having. "All they had to do was open the window and let out the smoke."

"Bet they're disappointed," she managed, taking another whiff of the clean air.

Far from it. First the landlady, Mrs. Rabineau, came over to thank Blair for taking such a risk, followed by all the other tenants. Taylor stayed by her mother's side, translating when necessary, but otherwise not saying much. When Blair finally had enough of breathing through a mask, she pulled it away and went solo in the afternoon air.

Outside of a little persistent coughing, she was okay. A little self-conscious about wearing a bathrobe in the front garden, but otherwise she was fine.

Everyone finally received permission to return to their apartments, and Blair and Taylor wandered along after them. Mounting the stairs to their own home, Blair kept an arm around Taylor, mostly because she needed the security of having her close.

Fires terrified her, and the possibility of losing Taylor in one just about stopped her heart. She hugged the young girl closer, and they pushed open the front door to a surprising scene.

Everything appeared normal. Except for a little smoke that lingered in the air, she couldn't tell by looking how close to disaster they'd come. Blair heard noises from the kitchen and went through the doorway to find one of the firemen doing something with the furnace.

"Do you have any idea how it started?" Blair asked, discovering he spoke English. Then she remembered Taylor had screamed something earlier...about it being her fault? She looked down at her daughter to find the tears were flowing again.

"I did it, Mom."

The fireman just raised an eyebrow and waited.

Blair hugged Taylor, doing her best to comfort the young girl before leading her to the high stool in the corner. Taylor jumped onto the seat, wiping the tears away as she tried to explain. Blair's heart went out to the child, but she maintained a calm front as she poured a tall glass of water and proceeded to drink it down.

Nothing would be gained by getting excited.

"I wanted to see if the brandy for the dessert would really light like you said it would. So I poured some in a bowl and threw a match in." She sobbed, brushing away the tears with a fist as she related the terrifying scene. "It scared me, kind of flared up and I guess I jumped or something, but I must have tipped the bowl over and the flames ran into the furnace and I threw some towels over it but that just made it worse...."

"And I think we can guess what happened after that, darling," Blair sighed. She coughed some more, drank some more water, then turned to the fireman. "How much damage did the fire do?"

"Very little," the fireman replied. "The flames only spread through the coal in the hopper, and while that part isn't supposed to burn, it really didn't hurt anything. It was more a case of the flames being in the wrong part of the furnace."

"So we got all excited for nothing?"

"No," he smiled, shaking his head at Blair's misunderstanding. "If you hadn't put the fire out, it would have spread to the cabinets. You did a good job with that extinguisher," he said, moving toward the door. "All you have to do now is have the furnace man clean this out, then we'll send someone over to check it. Outside of the smoke damage, you were pretty lucky."

Blair walked him to the front door, smiling when he reminded her to replace the extinguisher.

"Mom, am I in a lot of trouble?" Taylor asked from behind her.

"What do you think?"

"I think I'm probably grounded for the next year or so," she mumbled, throwing herself down onto the sofa. Blair let her mull it over for a while, moving through the house to open windows the firemen had missed. A good airing out and everything would be back to normal, she thought, then remembered the furnace needed some work. She called the landlady, who said she'd arrange it through her brother-in-law, then settled down on the couch beside Taylor.

"You made two mistakes today, Taylor," she began, trying to keep in perspective the relative lack of damage to the apartment. "First, you played with matches after being told not to. Second, you poured a flammable liquid on top of the furnace."

"I didn't know it would spill," she said, the tears brimming over as she remembered the flames. "It all happened so fast. And I never thought about the furnace at all. We always do stuff on top of it, and it was the only place left to work. The counter was full."

"We've used the top of the furnace to keep food warm and that's all," Blair pointed out. "I've never used it as a work surface. But that's not the point. You know I've told you a million times not to play with matches. Do you think you understand now?"

Taylor hung her head, sighed heavily, then looked Blair squarely in the eyes. "I did a terrible thing, Mom."

"And you were lucky this time," Blair said. Leaning over to put an arm around her shoulders, she suggested. "I think cleaning the kitchen is punishment enough. Think you can manage?"

Taylor hugged her tightly, then raced off through the doorway. Blair followed her and gave her instructions of what to do with the spoiled food and soot-covered cabinets, then wandered back to her bedroom where she glanced at the clock. She still had thirty minutes before Nick was due to arrive. It surprised her, especially when she realized the excitement of the fire and the aftermath had taken less than an hour.

Shrugging out of the robe, she stepped back into the shower and turned the water on high. It would take a long soaking to get the smell of smoke out of her hair, she mused, coughing as she turned her face to the warm steam of water. She coughed again, and realized the smoke in her lungs would take even longer to purge.

IT WOULDN'T HAVE HAPPENED in New Jersey, she realized.

Coal furnaces were a thing of the past in the States, whereas in Europe they could be found in many homes. Reaching out to shut off the water, Blair admitted that without the furnace, there probably wouldn't have been a fire.

She bent down to a low cabinet and pulled out a couple of dry towels, wrapping one around her hair and using the other to dry herself. Blair noticed the forgotten packet of lilac soap over on the sink, and debated taking another shower with it. But she couldn't summon the energy, and besides, it was getting late. Wrapping the towel around herself, she opened the bathroom door.

"Taylor told me all about it," Nick said. He was leaning against the wall opposite the bathroom door, obviously waiting for her to come out. "Why didn't you call me?"

"Because you were coming over anyway, and I guess I had other things on my mind," she said, securing the end of the towel across her breasts. She wondered briefly what Taylor had thought when Nick came into her bedroom, then noticed he'd left the door to the hallway open. That worked, she thought, realizing he wasn't here to do anything that Taylor couldn't see.

"Are you really okay, love?" he asked gruffly, his eyes doing a thorough check of anything and everything visible.

"I'm really okay," she said softly.

"Then come here so I can hold you."

"I told you I'm okay," she said.

"But I'm not," he growled. "Come here."

Blair took the steps that separated them and leaned into his solid warmth. It felt good to have his arms around her. Safe and secure.

It was where she always wanted to be.

They stood there for long moments, soaking in each other's warmth and reassurance. The towel around her hair finally slipped, and she reluctantly stepped back.

"I'll be out in a few minutes," she said, easing Nick toward the door. "Why don't you go keep Taylor company," she suggested. "I think she's feeling pretty low right now."

He nodded briefly, stroking her with his eyes in a fashion that awakened her senses and made her sway toward him. But he turned before she reached him, pulling the door closed behind him.

Blair sighed at her erratic reflexes, then moved to sit in front of the mirror. Picking up the brush, she started working on the tangled mess, but couldn't get enthused about the project. Setting it aside, she unscrewed the lid on a jar of moisturizer and worked it into her skin, covering every millimeter of her face before she was satisfied. Her skin glowed from the treatment, and she decided against using anything but a minimum of makeup. Blair added a stroke of blush, a little mascara, and called it quits before she picked up the hairbrush again.

As she struggled with the tangles, she thought about the fire—what had caused it, how likely it was to happen again. She really hadn't stopped thinking about it yet felt as if she'd been dream walking ever since she'd heard Taylor's first scream.

Although she knew for a fact that Taylor would never make the same mistake about matches, there was always the coal furnace to think about. It frightened her, even though Blair knew there was very little to back up her fears. Lots of people used coal furnaces, and almost none of them had experienced the disaster of a fire.

But logic aside, she knew she'd never be able to light it again. Which left her with a problem. They would have to move to a place that didn't have a coal furnace.

Somewhere like New Jersey.

CONTRARY TO NICK'S expectations, Blair didn't fight him over his suggestion that they not stay in the apartment that night.

"I used the last of the hot water for my shower anyway. I guess we'll be better off going to a hotel."

Blair was moving through the apartment, pulling the windows closed as the evening air began to chill. "I thought you could call over to your place and see if they have another room."

"Another room where?" Taylor asked from the kitchen doorway.

"At Nick's hotel," Blair supplied, wincing at the filthy clothes Taylor still wore. "Are you about finished with the kitchen?"

"For today, I think. It's taking a long time, especially 'cause I have to heat water on the stove."

Blair just smiled, refusing to feel guilty about her shower. "Nick suggested we stay at the hotel since there's no hot water. And I think it still smells of smoke, so we really don't have a choice, do we?"

"Can I stay over at Katherine's instead," Taylor asked, referring to a school chum who lived across town. "Then I can tell her all about the fire and about what a hero you were."

"I don't know about the hero part, but if her mom doesn't mind having you, it's okay with me." Tossing her a clean towel, she added, "But I doubt if she'll have you looking like that. Why don't you call her, then spend some time cleaning up."

Taylor used the telephone first, then handed it to Nick. In the meantime, Blair heated some water so Taylor wouldn't have to struggle too hard to wash off the dirt.

"She said it was okay." Taylor carried the pan of water back toward the bathroom, threatening to throw it over Nick when he teased her about her dirty face.

"I booked you a room," he said, waiting for the bathroom door to close. "But I'd rather you shared mine."

"Don't you think I've had enough excitement for one day?" she teased, allowing Nick to pull her into the circle of his arms.

"We've got the whole evening ahead of us," he murmured into her ear, nipping it lightly before moving to her lips. "You can give me your answer later."

Blair sighed against his mouth, feeling the excitement begin to build on top of her taut nerves. She hadn't been able to settle down yet, still had visions of the house going up in flames as they watched from the garden. But having Nick close was helping, and she closed her eyes and nestled closer to his warmth.

He accepted her invitation, covering her mouth with his, taking his time. She trembled, and he smoothed his palms over the muscles in her arms, soothing the tension from her body. He deepened his kiss, pressing her mouth open to accept his tongue, drawing it lightly over hers.

Blair rose onto her toes, needing to be closer, wanting to give him more. Her fingers tangled in the short curls just above his collar, then slid around the heated skin of his neck to toy with the knot of his tie.

Nick groaned and swept his hands down her back to the swell of her hips. He held her hard against him, savoring the sensation of her body arching against his before he pulled away. Dropping his head until his forehead rested on hers, he cautioned her in whispers. Blair giggled at his threats, sliding a quick glance toward the hallway before drawing the tip of her tongue over his lower lip.

He captured her with his teeth, biting gently until he heard a door slam. "Lucky for you her timing is so good," he kidded, moving across the room to stare out the window at a passing boat.

Taylor was packed and ready to go. With Peter Rabbit peeking out of her knapsack, she jumped on Nick's offer of a ride and hugged Blair good night. "You okay about everything, Mom?" she asked, catching her lip between her teeth in a nervous reflex.

Blair smiled. "I'm okay about everything."

With a few last-minute instructions, they were off. Blair set about getting her own things ready, then made a last check of the house. The kitchen still needed some work, but that could wait.

Blair heard Nick's footsteps on the stairway, and rushed out to meet him. It seemed as though she couldn't get out of there fast enough.

"ABOUT THE FIRE—"

"I'm really not in the mood for a lecture about it tonight, Nick," she warned. "And don't tell me how it wouldn't have happened if we didn't live in Europe, because I already know that." Blair poured herself another glass of water from the pitcher the waiter had left on their table and sipped it nervously.

"On the contrary," he said, uneasy with the anxious glances Blair had been shooting in his direction all evening. "A fire can happen anywhere, and from what Taylor told me, I thought you handled it very well."

"But this particular kind of fire wouldn't have happened in the States because hardly anyone has ever seen one of these coal furnaces, much less used one in their home," she said, parroting the words she knew he would say if she gave him a chance. "I know all that so you don't have to repeat it. This is just another example of the things people who live in New Jersey don't have to worry about."

"That's true, but you have to remember that this was just a freak accident," he reminded her. "But if you're really upset about it, you might want to consider replacing the furnace with gas or electricity. That is, if you plan on staying much longer in Bruges," he added, remembering Blair's penchant for moving. But he didn't pursue that topic, mostly because he got the idea she liked Bruges and hadn't given any thought to leaving yet.

He was counting on it.

The waiter interrupted with a platter of rich-looking desserts, and Blair recoiled at the sweet offering. Dessert wasn't something she wanted to think about, not tonight. She held her breath until Nick waved the man away, then let it out carefully.

"I was thinking of more drastic measures," she finally said, wondering why Nick was being so slow on the uptake tonight. He hadn't said any of the things she expected, although she'd waited all through dinner for him to get his shots in.

"Such as?" he prompted, raising his glass for a final taste of the sweet wine.

"Moving to New Jersey."

Nick thought he heard her say "moving to New Jersey," but shook his head as if to dispel the idea before smiling indulgently across the table at her. He wasn't surprised that he was finding it hard to concentrate, particularly in view of the meeting he had set up in Brussels for the next afternoon. He desperately wanted to tell Blair all about it, but didn't dare.

It would be much better to surprise her with the results instead.

"Sorry, love," he apologized. "My thoughts were somewhere else. I could have sworn you said something about moving to New Jersey."

"I did," she said crossly. "I said I'm thinking about moving to New Jersey."

It penetrated that time. But Nick couldn't immediately make any sense out of the words because it was the last thing he'd ever expected to hear from Blair's lips. *New Jersey?*

Maybe this was a joke. Nick shot her a calculating glance and was astonished to realize she was serious. The discovery rendered him speechless.

Blair withstood his scrutiny, then breathed a sigh of relief when he didn't immediately tear her apart with questions. There was something else that was part of this, the one thing that might convince him. She took a deep breath, swallowed and held his eyes in a solid gaze as she proposed to him.

"I want to marry you, Nick," she whispered. "I want to marry you and live in New Jersey."

"NOW SAY THAT AGAIN," he demanded, gripping her arms to swing her around to face him. "And louder this time. I want to be sure I'm not imagining things."

He was angry, she realized. Blair bit her lip to keep it from trembling. This was definitely not the reaction she'd expected. Surprise, yes, a little of that. Perhaps even a little pique. Nick was traditional enough to want to do the asking himself, but she'd made up her mind to settle things between them, and couldn't be bothered with doing the conventional thing . . . waiting for Nick to ask!

It never occurred to her that he'd be angry . . . or that he might say no.

Until now, that is. Caught between the stone wall abutting the canal and Nick crowding in from the other side, Blair considered retracting her words. But that wasn't possible, because she'd meant what she said.

"I said I want to marry you," she repeated, lifting a hand to his face, her fingers skimming over his lips. "Is that so hard to believe?" she asked softly. "You know I love you. It just suddenly seemed like the thing to say."

"And the part about New Jersey?" he pressed, watching her face for signs of weakening. "What did you mean?"

"I meant what I said, Nick," she said, a nervous laugh escaping her lips as her hand dropped to her side. "I said I want to move to New Jersey. I think it makes sense."

"You're wrong, Blair. It makes no sense at all."

"I don't understand." And she was suddenly afraid. It was going wrong, so terribly wrong. She trembled under his hold, flinching against the rough stones at her back. "I thought you loved me, too."

He didn't answer that.

Instead he let her go, backing away from her until he stood several feet away. Shoving his hands into his trouser pockets, he stood across the cobbled pathway and stared at her.

He'd thought everything was under control, but she was doing it to him again. Surprising him, making him rethink his plans, sending him signals that didn't make any sense whatsoever. Blair had been so vehement about wanting to stay in Europe. And now, in a total about face, she was proposing!

If she'd just waited another day, he sighed. One more day, and it wouldn't be happening this way.

Standing apart from her, it was easier to think. He watched as she turned away, leaning across the parapet to peer into the canal. The full skirt she wore teased the back of her legs, lifting in the breeze to tantalize him with hints of the curves beneath.

It suddenly dawned on him why she'd proposed . . . why she'd chosen this day, this time to commit herself to marriage. It was obvious, even though it had taken a few minutes to sink in. Nick wished he'd seen it coming so he could have avoided it, then Blair wouldn't be suffering the anxiety that was tearing her apart.

But he couldn't help what was already past. And, for a moment, he was almost afraid he wouldn't be able to fix it.

He had to try.

"Blair."

She turned her face to him, her fingers gripping the stones in a viselike hold.

"I want you to think about something," he began slowly, closing the distance between them. "And I want you to take your time, lots of time. I don't even want an answer until tomorrow night."

"What are you talking about?" she whispered.

"Mostly about what you said," he replied. "But also about what you didn't say."

In the fading light, he watched the play of emotions as they crossed her face. She really didn't know, he realized. And because of that, he softened his words. "I want to marry you, probably more than anything in the world."

She gasped, the sudden relief ripping through the pain and confusion as she understood what he'd said. But he touched her lips with his fingers, frustrating her attempts to speak.

"But I need to know if you're offering to move to New Jersey because you love me and want to be with me...or if you're running away from the fire...or from your life-style."

That was it, of course. The crux of the problem. As much as he loved Blair, he needed to know she loved him back. Everything else aside, their life together would only work if she honestly loved him.

Nick added his final demand. "And when you figure it out, I want you to convince me."

"If all—" she began, and this time it was his mouth that sealed her lips. He overpowered her, drinking in her cries of protest as he kept her from saying the words that were clamoring to come out.

And when she began to kiss him back, he loosened his hold. He rained light kisses over her upturned face, then returned to her lips to satisfy another hunger. Her hands crept up his chest, sliding upward until she could wrap then around his neck.

With his arms gently holding her close, Nick cherished her. He made love to her in a way neither had ever experienced before.

In a shaft of light from a nearby shop, he held her and kissed her and whispered words of love. Blair responded in kind, taking his kisses and giving him hers, holding him as urgently, as gently as he held her.

It was incredibly intimate, yet perfectly innocent.

It ended as gently as it had begun, and this time Blair didn't try to speak. Suddenly shy, she dipped her eyes and began to walk toward the hotel, taking his hand because she needed to touch him, to know he was there and not a dream.

13

SHE REACHED OUT to touch him, and he wasn't there.

She'd sat up and he'd vanished.

Blair collapsed against the pillows, her heartbeat still jumping at the illusion. She'd been dreaming again, she realized. Off and on, all night, she'd drifted in and out of a light sleep filled with dreams and phantoms.

Some of them had been good, a few of them disturbing. None of them were about the fire, and that probably surprised her more than anything. Reaching over to snap on the light, she fluffed up the pillows and sat up, sparing a few choice words for Nick's insistence that they spend the night separately.

She wouldn't be dreaming at all if he were here... where he belonged.

The dreams were all about Nick, of course. Life with him, life without him...and all the variations. It didn't take an analyst to tell her that, and Blair felt sure that a couple of them would make interesting studies. Like the one about Nick and Taylor waterskiing across the Market plaza, shrieking challenges at each other as they raced over the cobblestones behind Frankie's carriage.

Nick had been right to question her motives, she knew. Until she'd thought about it, she hadn't realized how desperate she must have sounded. It was the overreaction to the fire that had triggered the proposal, but now she was left with a mess to clean up.

If he expected her to take it back, then he was in for a surprise.

All she had to think about now was how to convince him she knew what she was doing. That part was beginning to worry her, mostly because Nick wasn't exactly a pushover.

But then, he'd never given her a chance to be really creative . . . and that could *really* make a difference.

NICK CAUGHT SIGHT of Taylor as he rounded the corner, just a few yards down from the Market plaza. She was selling something again, he thought, then changed his mind as he noticed her pushing the goods on a passerby without demanding payment.

"Hi, midget."

Taylor shrieked, her stricken face bloodred as she twisted to face him. Following along the same lines as the shriek, she crossed her forearms over her chest and dashed off in the opposite direction, screaming something unintelligible at the top of her lungs.

Strange, he thought, pausing for just a moment to think about it. Taylor was usually glad to see him. Still, he had been gone for almost a full day. Perhaps she was going through one of those growing stages and he'd missed the kickoff.

Shrugging away the trifling aberration, Nick resumed his pace. Blair had left a note that she'd meet him in the Market, and he was anxious to share his news.

He was also interested to hear what conclusions she'd arrived at over the past twenty-four hours. He'd given her an ultimatum, designed to make her commit herself totally and without any other reason than that she loved him.

In return, Nick intended to save her from New Jersey. Or save New Jersey from Blair—whichever way you wanted to look at it. That was his commitment, one he intended to keep.

He hoped Taylor's odd behavior wouldn't distract them from settling things.

The crowd grew more dense as he made his way out of the side street and into the Market proper. Once there, Nick started taking more notice of the people around him.

It was difficult to ignore them anymore, and he wondered irrelevantly how he'd made it this far without noticing there was something distinctly odd about how they were dressed.

It was odd because there was an astounding number of people wearing T-shirts with the slogan I LOVE NEW JERSEY emblazoned on the front. And when a horse-drawn carriage meandered by, Nick couldn't help but wonder how they'd managed to get the T-shirt on the horse.

"There must be two or three hundred people wearing those things," he said, feeling her before he saw her.

Blair tucked her hand into the crook of his elbow and led him across the Market toward Leo's flower stand. "More like four hundred," she said. "At least, that's how many we made."

"I don't suppose you told them why they're doing this?" he asked, reaching for her hand and wrapping it in his long fingers as he concentrated on not looking at her. Just having her beside him was enough. His eyes could feast on her later, when no one was watching his reactions.

For now, it seemed as though they were onstage—certainly no place to declare his everlasting love. But then, how many people couldn't guess?

"Sure I told them," she said, laughing at his chagrin. "Everyone loves a love story, especially on a late spring day in one of the most romantic cities in Europe."

"So what's next in the script?" he asked, shaking Leo's hand as they approached the stall. "Do they want me on my knees?"

"They might not, but I kind of like the idea," she teased, gasping in surprise when he fell to one knee in front of her.

Leo bowed before the scene, presenting Blair with a massive bouquet and an enthusiastic hug. Nick waited, watching her easy acceptance of the affection, knowing there was nothing in this world that would make him take Blair away from her life here.

He saw the T-shirt Blair was wearing then, and a slow smile lit his face. I LOVE NICK was on the front, and she twisted to give him the rear view, which read I *WILL* LOVE NEW JERSEY. He grabbed her hand and planted a very noisy, very wet kiss on her knuckles, playing the ham and enjoying himself immensely. He didn't need to say anything—it wouldn't have been possible anyway. The audience was having great fun shouting their own suggestions, stealing the best lines from all the romantic poets in their efforts to prompt him. Finally, after much hooting and prompting, he let her pull him from his knees, but not before the gathering crowd applauded their appreciation.

Blair finally had the grace to blush, and she dragged him through the crowd of well-wishers and curious onlookers toward a waiting carriage.

And, for the first time since Taylor had shouted out the alarm that Nick was approaching, Blair was nervous.

"I should have remembered that you don't take challenges lightly," he murmured, draping an arm over her shoulder and pulling her back against the leather cushions.

Snuggled safely in his arms, she lost her nervousness. "It wasn't so much the challenge itself as it was the greater principle."

"Greater principle?" he repeated, raising a hand to stroke her cheek. It was so soft there, he thought. So soft everywhere. He pulled a lavender rose from the bouquet in her lap, drawing the delicate petals across her lips, tickling her nose with the heady scent.

Blair sighed under his caress, struggling to make herself explain when all she wanted was to curl up in his arms and watch the world go by. But she persevered, and soon found herself presenting a logical explanation to what she had designated as "The Great T-Shirt Expo."

"The greater principle being how much I love you and that I finally figured out that where we live makes no difference whatsoever. As long as we can be together, nothing else matters."

"Seems like that's how Taylor feels about her relationship with you," he said softly. "At least, it always looked that way to me."

"If you had pointed that out yesterday, I wouldn't be out four hundred T-shirts," she said dryly, punching him playfully in the side.

The carriage passed through the narrow streets, pausing occasionally for traffic, carrying them beside the picturesque canal where swans were paddling in the almost still water.

"Do you really think you'll love New Jersey?" he asked, cupping his fingers to lift her chin.

"I'll try," she said honestly. "I'm sure that once I put my mind to it, it'll be a cinch. I don't even care if you have a house with a coal furnace," she said, then shot an anxious look at him. "You don't, do you?"

"It doesn't matter," he said, chuckling at her consternation.

"Of course, it doesn't matter," Blair agreed. "I've already told you I'll love you anywhere." And she lifted her lips for that first kiss, the one she'd been waiting for all day long.

Nick lowered his head, just barely touching her mouth with his as he popped the question. "Will you mind terribly if I decide not to take you to New Jersey after all?"

Her heart stood still and she was suddenly afraid that she'd lost. But he was kissing her, his lips plying hers apart to gain entrance for his hungry tongue. Blair accepted the caress automatically, stunned by his words.

"I thought Bruges might suit us better." And he kissed her again, massaging the slick heat of her mouth with his tongue, relearning her secrets, teaching her that love was everything.

Blair bit his tongue, not very hard, but enough to get his attention. "Talk or die," she threatened, holding the bouquet up as if it were a blunt instrument.

"That meeting I had in Brussels today was the last of a series I've been holding with a Belgian company. We've agreed to open a branch of my company here— well, the site is closer to Brussels actually, but I thought we could live in Bruges."

"How can you do business here?" she demanded. "You don't speak French or Flemish or anything!"

"But I speak English, and that's adequate for my purposes. After all, it is the language of science."

"So we don't have to go to New Jersey?" she asked, breathless at the turn events had taken.

"Not now," he agreed. "Perhaps there will come a time later when it will be necessary, but for the next few years, I'm pretty committed to getting our research started here."

She didn't protest as Nick drew down the hand holding the bouquet, didn't even mind when he pried her fingers from the crushed stems and placed them on the seat. And when he pulled her into his arms, she slid her own hands up to his shoulders.

"You mean I went through all this for nothing?"

"Of course not. You needed to know something about yourself, about our relationship, and you found it out. I don't call that wasted effort."

"What do you call your underhanded methods?" she asked, drawing a shallow breath as she waited for his answer.

"Compromise, my love," he breathed just moments before claiming her lips. "Compromise."

"YOU MEAN we did all this for nothing!"

Taylor flopped back against the facing seat, pretending a disgust with the same lousy technique Blair had tried. But the smile that kept popping up at the edge of her lips betrayed her true feelings, and it didn't take long for her to abandon her indignant pose.

"I suppose if you really want to live in New Jersey..." Nick offered, his face a study in sincerity.

·"No!" mother and daughter chorused, readily dismissing his suggestion.

The carriage slowed, and Taylor shouted something to the driver that started them on another round of the Market. They'd been circling the plaza for some time now, long enough for Taylor to have jumped on and joined in the celebration. Typically she'd taken the announcement in stride, zeroing in on the finer points that neither Nick nor Blair had yet considered.

"It's a good thing you're marrying him now, Mom," Taylor said. "Another couple of years and you'll be too old to have any more kids."

Nick and Blair choked in unison, then eyed each other cautiously. Kids? Blair thought. Where did Taylor get those ideas!

"You think I'm almost over the hill, do you?" Babies, she thought, wondering if Nick would mind having a couple of more mouths to feed. She segued into an image of Nick coaxing a spoon of oatmeal into the mouth of a towheaded infant, and she smiled broadly. Perhaps an unpredictable child was just the thing Nick needed.

"Well, you're not getting any younger," Taylor pointed out. "And Nick's even older than you are."

"I don't think it's the same problem, midget," he managed, smothering the urge to open a debate on age and parenting. It wasn't that the subject of babies— singular or plural—was beyond the realm of his imagination, but he thought he should clear it with Blair first before discussing the possibility with her daughter.

Taylor responded to his silence with a giggle, and Nick found himself searching the skyline for rescue.

It came in the form of a delegation of Blair's friends.

Dressed in T-shirts that said I LOVE BRUGES, they surrounded the carriage, joining hands as they serenaded the new family. The driver translated the Flemish love song, and joined in for a rousing chorus.

Blair snuggled deeper into Nick's warmth, reveling in the peace and security he brought her. And when he reached across the aisle to pull Taylor against his other side, her world was complete.

Epilogue

"YOU NEVER ACTUALLY asked me to marry you," she said without taking her eyes off the band of gold that encircled the third finger of her left hand.

Nick rolled over and captured that hand, bringing it to his lips for a quick nibble. When his teeth latched on to her wedding ring, Blair jerked her hand back and hid it under the pillow.

"Don't you think it's a little late to be proposing?" he asked, watching with pleasure as his fingers slid across the bare skin of her hip.

"Not if you value your marriage," she retorted, drawing herself into a kneeling position just inches out of his reach. Catching the hot look in his eyes, Blair belatedly pulled the sheet up to cover her breasts.

"I went down on my knees for you!" he insisted, calculating the force needed to snatch the sheet out of her grasp.

"So the hard part's over."

"What more do you want?" he prodded, slowly wrapping the end of the sheet around his fist.

"The words, darling. Give me the words," she said silkily. "And an engagement ring would be nice," she teased, not in the least bit serious about it.

"Greedy!" he accused, surreptitiously sliding a hand into the top drawer of the bedside table. His fingers wrapped around a small box before emerging.

Blair missed it all, diverted by the hungry wanting that filled his eyes. Nick pushed himself up on one elbow, keeping the sheet secured in one hand as he snapped open the box with the other, holding it in his palm for her inspection.

Her eyes grew round at the sight of the sparkling jewel, and she hesitantly reached out a single finger to touch it. "It's beautiful," she whispered, not daring to remove it from the box.

"You're beautiful," he countered, then pulled it from the velvet cushion as he tightened his grip on the sheet. In a single coordinated movement, he pulled the sheet from her body and pushed Blair down to the pillows. "I want you to wear this because I love you," he murmured, slipping it on to her finger before following her down. He kissed her then, long and hard, sealing their commitment with a promise of eternal love.

It was later, much later, when she remembered he still hadn't proposed. But somehow it didn't seem important.

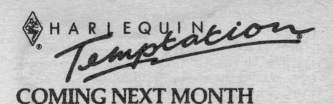

COMING NEXT MONTH

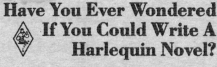

Have You Ever Wondered If You Could Write A Harlequin Novel?

Here's great news—Harlequin is offering a series of cassette tapes to help you do just that. Written by Harlequin editors, these tapes give practical advice on how to make your characters—and your story—come alive. There's a tape for each contemporary romance series Harlequin publishes.

Mail order only

All sales final

TO: *Harlequin Reader Service*
Audiocassette Tape Offer
P.O. Box 1396
Buffalo, NY   14269-1396

I enclose a check/money order payable to HARLEQUIN READER SERVICE® for $9.70 ($8.95 plus 75¢ postage and handling) for EACH tape ordered for the total sum of $_____*
Please send:

☐ Romance and Presents   ☐ Intrigue
☐ American Romance   ☐ Temptation
☐ Superromance   ☐ All five tapes ($38.80 total)

Signature_____
                                                    (please print clearly)
Name:_____
Address:_____
State:_____ Zip:_____

*Iowa and New York residents add appropriate sales tax.

                                                    AUDIO-H

INDULGE A LITTLE SWEEPSTAKES
OFFICIAL RULES

SWEEPSTAKES RULES AND REGULATIONS. NO PURCHASE NECESSARY.

1. NO PURCHASE NECESSARY. To enter complete the official entry form and return with the invoice in the envelope provided. Or you may enter by printing your name, complete address and your daytime phone number on a 3 x 5 piece of paper. Include with your entry the hand printed words "Indulge A Little Sweepstakes." Mail your entry to: Indulge A Little Sweepstakes, P.O. Box 1397, Buffalo, NY 14269-1397. No mechanically reproduced entries accepted. Not responsible for late, lost, misdirected mail, or printing errors.

2. Three winners, one per month (Sept. 30, 1989, October 31, 1989 and November 30, 1989), will be selected in random drawings. All entries received prior to the drawing date will be eligible for that month's prize. This sweepstakes is under the supervision of MARDEN-KANE, INC. an independent judging organization whose decisions are final and binding. Winners will be notified by telephone and may be required to execute an affidavit of eligibility and release which must be returned within 14 days, or an alternate winner will be selected.

3. Prizes: 1st Grand Prize (1) a trip for two to Disneyworld in Orlando, Florida. Trip includes round trip air transportation, hotel accommodations for seven days and six nights, plus up to $700 expense money (ARV $3,500). 2nd Grand Prize (1) a seven-night Chandris Caribbean Cruise for two includes transportation from nearest major airport, accommodations, meals plus up to $1,000 in expense money (ARV $4,300). 3rd Grand Prize (1) a ten day Hawaiian holiday for two includes round trip air transportation for two, hotel accommodations, sightseeing, plus up to $1,200 in spending money (ARV $7,700). All trips subject to availability and must be taken as outlined on the entry form.

4. Sweepstakes open to residents of the U.S. and Canada 18 years or older except employees and the families of Torstar Corp., its affiliates, subsidiaries and Marden-Kane, Inc. and all other agencies and persons connected with conducting this sweepstakes. All Federal, State and local laws and regulations apply. Void wherever prohibited or restricted by law. Taxes, if any are the sole responsibility of the prize winners. Canadian winners will be required to answer a skill testing question. Winners consent to the use of their name, photograph and/or likeness for publicity purposes without additional compensation.

5. For a list of prize winners, send a stamped, self-addressed envelope to Indulge A Little Sweepstakes Winners, P.O. Box 701, Sayreville, NJ 08871.

© 1989 HARLEQUIN ENTERPRISES LTD.

DL-SWPS

INDULGE A LITTLE SWEEPSTAKES
OFFICIAL RULES

SWEEPSTAKES RULES AND REGULATIONS. NO PURCHASE NECESSARY.

1. NO PURCHASE NECESSARY. To enter complete the official entry form and return with the invoice in the envelope provided. Or you may enter by printing your name, complete address and your daytime phone number on a 3 x 5 piece of paper. Include with your entry the hand printed words "Indulge A Little Sweepstakes." Mail your entry to: Indulge A Little Sweepstakes, P.O. Box 1397, Buffalo, NY 14269-1397. No mechanically reproduced entries accepted. Not responsible for late, lost, misdirected mail, or printing errors.

2. Three winners, one per month (Sept. 30, 1989, October 31, 1989 and November 30, 1989), will be selected in random drawings. All entries received prior to the drawing date will be eligible for that month's prize. This sweepstakes is under the supervision of MARDEN-KANE, INC. an independent judging organization whose decisions are final and binding. Winners will be notified by telephone and may be required to execute an affidavit of eligibility and release which must be returned within 14 days, or an alternate winner will be selected.

3. Prizes: 1st Grand Prize (1) a trip for two to Disneyworld in Orlando, Florida. Trip includes round trip air transportation, hotel accommodations for seven days and six nights, plus up to $700 expense money (ARV $3,500). 2nd Grand Prize (1) a seven-night Chandris Caribbean Cruise for two includes transportation from nearest major airport, accommodations, meals plus up to $1,000 in expense money (ARV $4,300). 3rd Grand Prize (1) a ten day Hawaiian holiday for two includes round trip air transportation for two, hotel accommodations, sightseeing, plus up to $1,200 in spending money (ARV $7,700). All trips subject to availability and must be taken as outlined on the entry form.

4. Sweepstakes open to residents of the U.S. and Canada 18 years or older except employees and the families of Torstar Corp., its affiliates, subsidiaries and Marden-Kane, Inc. and all other agencies and persons connected with conducting this sweepstakes. All Federal, State and local laws and regulations apply. Void wherever prohibited or restricted by law. Taxes, if any are the sole responsibility of the prize winners. Canadian winners will be required to answer a skill testing question. Winners consent to the use of their name, photograph and/or likeness for publicity purposes without additional compensation.

5. For a list of prize winners, send a stamped, self-addressed envelope to Indulge A Little Sweepstakes Winners, P.O. Box 701, Sayreville, NJ 08871.

© 1989 HARLEQUIN ENTERPRISES LTD.

DL-SWPS

INDULGE A LITTLE—WIN A LOT!

Summer of '89 Subscribers-Only Sweepstakes

OFFICIAL ENTRY FORM

This entry must be received by: October 31, 1989
This month's winner will be notified by: Nov. 7, 1989
Trip must be taken between: Dec. 7, 1989–April 7, 1990
(depending on sailing schedule)

YES, I want to win the Caribbean cruise vacation for two! I understand the prize includes round-trip airfare, a one-week cruise including private cabin and all meals, and a daily allowance as revealed on the "Wallet" scratch-off card.

Name_____

Address_____

City_____State/Prov._____Zip/Postal Code_____

Daytime phone number_____
Area code

Return entries with invoice in envelope provided. Each book in this shipment has two entry coupons—and the more coupons you enter, the better your chances of winning!
© 1989 HARLEQUIN ENTERPRISES LTD.

DINDL-2

INDULGE A LITTLE—WIN A LOT!

Summer of '89 Subscribers-Only Sweepstakes

OFFICIAL ENTRY FORM

This entry must be received by: October 31, 1989
This month's winner will be notified by: Nov. 7, 1989
Trip must be taken between: Dec. 7, 1989–April 7, 1990
(depending on sailing schedule)

YES, I want to win the Caribbean cruise vacation for two! I understand the prize includes round-trip airfare, a one-week cruise including private cabin and all meals, and a daily allowance as revealed on the "Wallet" scratch-off card.

Name_____

Address_____

City_____State/Prov._____Zip/Postal Code_____

Daytime phone number_____
Area code

Return entries with invoice in envelope provided. Each book in this shipment has two entry coupons—and the more coupons you enter, the better your chances of winning!
© 1989 HARLEQUIN ENTERPRISES LTD.

DINDL-2